THE EVER FIEND

TALON STORMBRINGER

RANDY ELLEFSON

Llurien Books
GAITHERSBURG, MARYLAND

Evermore Press, LLC
Gaithersburg, Maryland
www.evermorepress.org

Publisher's Note: This book is a work of fiction. All names, characters, locations, and incidents are products of the author's imagination, or have been used fictitiously. Any semblance to actual persons living or dead, locales, or events is entirely coincidental and not intended by the author.

Publisher's Cataloging-In-Publication Data
(Prepared by The Donohue Group, Inc.)

Names: Ellefson, Randy, author.
Title: The ever fiend / Randy Ellefson.
Description: 1st ed. | Gaithersburg, Maryland : Llurien
    Books, [2016] | Series: Talon Stormbringer ; [1]
Identifiers: ISBN 9781946995629 (paperback) |
    ISBN 9781946995476 (hardcover) |
    ISBN 9781946995483 (ebook)
Subjects: LCSH: Swordsmen--Fiction. | Wizards--Fiction. |
    Magic--Fiction. | Imaginary places--Fiction. | LCGFT:
    Paranormal fiction. | Fantasy fiction.
Classification: LCC PS3605.L431 E94 2016 (print) | LCC
    PS3605.L431 (ebook) | DDC 813/.6--dc23

CONTENTS

ACKNOWLEDGEMENTS

Special thanks to Jean Hall, Clayton Clement, and
Christopher Candice for their input

Edited by Niyati Joshi and JJ Henke

Cover design by Miblart

Maps by Randy Ellefson

Partial Map of the Kingdom of Illiandor, continent Antaria,
on the world of Llurien
http://www.llurien.com/continents/antaria/

CHAPTER ONE

THE WHITE TOWER

While most in Talendor slumbered, Talon Stormbringer crept through a hallway dark with moving shadows, his human ears and eyes alert. He'd already slipped undetected past a jhaikan and a mynx, undeterred by their ferocity and taste for man-flesh. Even the dozen sleeping riven in the courtyard hadn't given him pause, though fully armored knights would have turned away. The little monsters were infamous for stirring at the slightest sound, waking to become a whirling dervish of steel. Talon had been known to unleash the same from the sword gripped in one hand.

Now he heard nothing, not even his own passage, the supple black leather pants and tunic he wore never squeaking as he crept toward the doorway and his prize. The gold figurine of a great bird of prey, said to be magical and worth a fortune, awaited. Stories in taverns had piqued his interest but had also warned him of the dangers. The greatest of those was the wizard whose white tower he now prowled. Some said Viland Shadowbreaker enjoyed unsavory habits when few were looking, his public persona of benevolent charm masking a dark truth.

Talon reached the open doorway at the hall's end and peered in. Four torches cast their light along the walls. He shook his head at the obvious trap. No one would light so many torches for a room that held nothing but a pedestal, upon which sat the figurine, light glinting off its golden curves. A room without a lock much less a door could ensnare only a fool. And each of the earlier dangers he'd passed had offered an easy way around for a skilled thief like himself. The question was why Viland wanted to capture someone. Talon didn't intend to find out.

He sheathed his sword, then slipped a light rope from his waist, fashioning a loop on one end. Lassoing wasn't a skill he had spent much time mastering, but at the fourth attempt he managed to get it around the statue. A gentle tug, and the loop tightened. With a quick jerk he brought the figurine flying through the air to him. He deftly caught it and deposited it into a cloth sack. He hefted his sword, and with a smirk, turned back the way he had come.

"Astiana mer," said the silky, sophisticated voice behind him.

Talon froze more at the magic words than at the realization that a man was there. He tried to turn again but found that he could not. For all his strength, he could neither move his arms nor the powerful muscles of his legs. Like a statue he stood, imposing in his might, steel-gray eyes smoldering with indignation. The breeze from a nearby open window did not stir the golden hair around his broad shoulders, even though he felt the wind on his face and heard it crackle the torches that sent his shadow down the hall. Joining that shadow were two others—one tall, one short—as quiet footsteps approached from behind.

"Don't worry," said the man. "It's temporary. And you can still talk." When Talon didn't speak, the wizard sighed and said, "Mer astiana."

Suddenly freed, Talon squeezed his sword, flexed his limbs, and weighed some options. Quick as he was, his blade would never reach the wizard before another spell stopped him, for no sword could fly faster than words. And while the taller shadow was likely the wizard, he had no idea to whom or what the other shadow belonged. He had to know before launching an attack. Besides, he could hardly assess foes with his back to them. He slowly turned around, scowling.

A black-robed, balding man stood beside the empty pedestal, a reassuring smile on his swarthy face. Perhaps he was a Marulan from across the Antaran Sea. But Marulans were thought to be mostly savages, their skins as black as their deeds, and not wizards with an air of sophistication and opulence. The man did not have an accent that Talon could hear. The long face, nose, and limbs matched what Talon had heard from stories. The dark eyes of Viland Shadowbreaker observed him coolly.

Beside Viland stood a karelia, all four and a half feet of him covered in dusky black plate armor, the sigil of a flaming sword emblazoned on his chest. Black hair swept back into a tight ponytail and pointed ears accentuated the impression of efficient speed, which drew Talon's eyes to the sheathed, curved sword at the karelia's hip. For a pleasant species, he seemed uncommonly sinister, the delicate features at odds with the cocky menace upon them. The translucent lorenia lines, which all karelia were born with, streaked across his cheeks as if fleeing the blue eyes toward his jugular. That the lines faintly glowed blue told Talon that something supernatural was still at play here, or he would have been unable to see the lines from five paces.

"You are brave to release your hold on me," Talon said, testing Viland's grasp of the situation.

"No games, warrior. You were smart enough to use that lasso, and you're smart enough to know I can kill you long before you reach me."

No kerr shit, thought Talon approvingly. He had little patience for fools. "So what now?"

"You've passed my test and—"

"How is being caught a success?"

"That figurine is only a lure to test the bravery of the ambitious. Few will attempt the perils to reach it."

The swordsman shrugged. "Your dangers weren't that dangerous."

"I don't need heroes, just uncommon men. You'll do nicely."

Talon's eyes narrowed in annoyance. He didn't care for being someone's pawn. That he had fallen into a trap, despite knowing it existed, also grated on his nerves. "For what?"

Viland raised a hand, palm outward. "In a moment. I am no threat to you. I give you my word that, if you refuse my offer, I will blank your memory of this night and drop you on a ship bound for Llorus, rather than kill you."

"Sounds like a lot of trouble."

"It's less trouble dragging your living body from my home than your dead one. I would rather avoid attention. Besides, I am not a murderer. And I assume you'd prefer not being killed or seeing a Solon Judge after your theft. Now, if you'll accept my offer?"

"Let's hear it."

From his pocket, the wizard pulled a small vial of brightly glowing, silver liquid that cast dancing shadows around the room. "This is silver elixir, one of the most potent elements on Llurien. I need more. You will get it for me."

Talon suspected the dangers of doing so were far worse than losing his memory, but he'd never heard of the stuff and wasn't sure he wanted to know what people did with it. "From where?"

"The Ever Pathways."

Talon snorted. "They don't exist. I may be young but I don't believe in children's tales."

"Yes, you are young. Eighteen winters?"

"Not even that." Even years earlier, his size and bearing had often inspired assumptions that he was a man already. If that meant making his own way and being no stranger to the finer delights of women, he qualified.

"Maybe that accounts for your bravery. You'll have need of it. I assure you, Everland is real."

"And so is the Ever Fiend?" Talon laughed. "I conquered my fear of him at three."

Now the karelia spoke with condescension that was clear despite the almost child-like pitch of his voice. "Your fear will return if you catch sight of him."

Seeing that Talon was unimpressed, and unconvinced, the wizard said, "Being prepared means knowing the truth. Lies and illusion raise your risk of failure. I don't want more damned souls wandering the Ever Pathways. They're an obstacle to my designs."

He spoke words of magic and stretched out one hand toward Talon as if to grasp his forehead from afar. Talon took one step back before the room disappeared and his mind's eye filled with visions. A dark landscape with stormy clouds and eerie light. A black tower precariously perched beside the crumbling edge of an enormous crevasse, mist rising from its depths. Stunted trees with bone white trunks beside a pool of shining liquid. Shadowy figures furtively moving just out of sight. And a robed, hooded figure that suddenly appeared between them, sending them fleeing with shrieks of terror.

The visions stopped and Talon realized he'd raised his sword. The karelia's lorenia lines glowed brighter than before but faded as he watched. Talon lowered the blade and asked, "How do I know that these visions are not an illusion?"

Viland replied, "Once you enter the paths, you will see."

Realizing he would get no further, Talon asked, "And what do I get out of this, aside from keeping my memories?" Nothing of great importance had happened recently so that he was desperate to recall it, but allowing a wizard to tamper with his mind didn't sit well with him. That Viland had already done so without his permission strengthened Talon's resolve to prevent it from happening again.

"Anything you find on the Everway is yours to keep," said Viland, watching Talon's eyes drop to the vial, "but you may not take some of the elixir for yourself."

"What's to stop me?"

"It can only be contained in vials made from Ever Sand, and you will return the ones I give you. And then there's my sorelia." He nodded at the karelia beside him and any trace of amusement fell from Talon's face.

The sorelian race, though physically identical to the karelian species to which it belongs, is malevolent whereas the karelia are benevolent. Sorelia use the supernatural skills granted by the gods for dark purposes. They keep to themselves apart from the rest of Llurien, holed up in the Sorelian Forest not too far north of Talendor. Talon had never seen a sorelia before, at least that he knew of. Perhaps the sneer should've made him realize.

That Viland had a sorelia working with him suggested that the stories of his nefarious living were true. Sending a sorelia into the Ever Pathways could only bring evil on the world. Maybe Talon needed to ensure that this mission failed and that he escaped with his life. There was no telling what this wizard would do with the silver elixir once he had it. Having his memory wiped now almost seemed like the better alternative than getting involved with this, but then Viland would just get another man for the job. Talon didn't want someone with far fewer scruples than himself helping these two. He might've been a thief of late, but he only stole from those who could afford to lose what he took. That reminded him of something.

"You want me to risk my life," Talon began, "for the chance to find discarded baubles on the Pathways?"

"A bauble here is a prize there," Viland answered smoothly. "Anything magical left inside for too long becomes enhanced, and even ordinary items can become special."

Talon's eyes narrowed. "The place is chaos, the rumors say, as is everything from there."

The sorelia grinned without humor. "He is smarter than he looks," he said. "Indeed, warrior, Everland is chaos. Do not put on any armor or clothing found inside or you might never remove it. Weapons, however, are often advantageous, albeit hard to predict. Still, the danger is to the one struck, not to the wielder."

"I don't need the help."

"Suit yourself. He's Nyborian," the sorelia remarked to Viland, referring to Talon's hometown a week's ride northeast. "The accent is subtle, but I hear the influence of the wagon peoples of Lorne to the east."

Talon pursed his lips. He didn't like anyone knowing too much about him, though little could come of that. The wizard seemed to feel the same way, having shrugged indifferently until he noticed the claw on a leather cord around Talon's neck. Then he perked up and remarked in surprise, "Talon Stormbringer. I should've recognized you sooner. I'm delighted. Your reputation precedes you."

"As does yours, Viland Shadowbreaker."

Talon had hoped to keep his name to himself while in Talendor, a city that was twin to the kingdom's capital, Illiandor, across the bay. Beyond that lay Nybor, where he'd lived with his parents until a jhaikan killed them; Talon had killed the beast and taken a claw to remember them by, then fled the memories. Someone had since seen the claw around his neck and called him Talon. The name had stuck, but he should've dropped the surname. Too late now. He had no family left in Nybor, and the brotherhood of knights to which his father had belonged didn't need to know about the dishonor he had brought upon his father by stealing for a living. Hopefully they'd never find out.

He asked the wizard, "If you need someone brave, why not send your pet jhaikan from the courtyard?"

"It's not real, for one," Viland replied, "but the Ever Fiend has a special hatred for jhaikan and that would invite trouble."

"As if this whole mission doesn't."

The legendary Ever Pathways could transport people from one place on Llurien to another in days instead of weeks, but few travelers made it out alive, and those who did had often gone insane. The karelia had eventually invented the Moon Gates to use the Ever Pathways at such speeds that one could traverse Llurien in an instant and bypass the dangers, but some still used Everland and the Ever Gates, such as the wizard standing before Talon now, black eyes glittering with forbidden knowledge.

Viland smiled. "The riven were also an illusion, but the mynx was not and will accompany you."

Talon raised an eyebrow, unsure the large feline could handle the terrors of Everland. "Battle trained?"

"Yes. Few animals have the courage to enter the pathways, but this one is unique. Noren here is his master." Viland nodded at the sorelia, who smirked.

Taking an animal, however tested, into a land of chaos didn't seem smart, but he had killed a rabid jaegar once and didn't doubt he could do the same to this mynx if it got out of control.

"You accept?" Viland asked, eyes gleaming.

Talon sighed. "When do we leave?"

CHAPTER TWO

EVERLAND

An hour later, Talon stood in the wide courtyard, the limestone wall he had climbed earlier surrounding him. Beyond that stood the few towers and homes tall enough to look down on him, though he couldn't see them anymore. To keep prying eyes away, the wizard had summoned a thick mist that hung above their heads, a breeze from the nearby Antaran Sea tugging at it. The cover wouldn't last long. On the stones around them were a wagon, empty crates, bulging sacks, and whatever mundane items Viland needed to run his home.

A stand of Siaran oaks and white Talana trees filled one corner, leaves trembling. Viland had assured him that the entrance to the Ever Pathways stood hidden behind them, invisible until it was opened. Only a spell could reveal the presence of a closed entrance. Karelia, who saw all manner of things few others could or would want to see, could even see one without trying to.

The sorelia, Noren, stood dressed as before, seemingly unmindful of the enormous sable mynx lying at his diminutive feet. Dark green patches dotted the cat's fur, visible only where it wasn't covered by plate armor on its back and sides. The half-green, half-black face, with a straight line down the center, made the maneless feline look distinctive. So did its unusual size—nearly as big as a horse—that indicated it was a male. Talon knew he would have to mind his tongue around the cat, for once bonded to a master, a mynx was fiercely loyal. If Talon spoke rudely to Noren, the sorelia wouldn't have to issue a command for the mynx to kill Talon; the mynx might do it on its own. And if Noren died in there, the cat could become trouble.

The others accompanying them were less impressive. One seemed to be an ordinary swordsman save for the cockiness in his stance and eyes, as if he wanted to dare Talon to swordplay but had thought better of it for the latter's size. Beside him and looking regal in gray plate mail stood a knight whose dour expression suggested little interest in this affair. His haunted eyes lingered instead on a dark-haired woman, who wore black leather and two short swords at her hips. She stood with more confidence than the knight or the swordsman. Surpassing them all in nonchalance was a male kryll, a species known for their mastery of physical combat, whether by hand or with weapons. He lounged catlike against the wall, a jhaikanstaff resting in the crook of his arm. Six of them, plus the cat, would enter Everland.

Talon knew nothing about them except that none were Ever Walkers—a group of individuals who voluntarily walked the Ever Pathways to seek fortune. He'd asked Viland about this only to be informed that Ever Walkers had been banned in the Kingdom of Illiandor and were hard to come by as a result. Besides, the wizard preferred not relying on people with an allegiance to someone other than himself, even if the Ever Walkers were more qualified for the risks involved. Not for the first time, Talon wondered what had happened to the man he was likely replacing, for he sensed this wasn't their first foray into Everland.

"How do we get to this silver elixir?" he asked Viland, who handed him a sash to wear from one shoulder to the opposite hip. It held six black vials, each corked but empty and with small handles.

"Noren will find the Poison Pond," the wizard answered, "where the waters are the elixir. He has been there before. You are to follow his lead."

"Poison Pond?"

Viland smiled without humor. "No one knows if it's truly poison, but riven were found floating in it once and it was assumed they'd died from drinking the enchanted waters. I suspect they merely drowned."

"Riven can't swim," Talon remarked. The diminutive species was too lazy to learn much of anything. With bodies consumed by one disease or another, it was entirely possible that their decaying flesh had poisoned the waters.

"Indeed. The question then is why would they enter the pool? The Ever Fiend is believed to sip from it and might have approached, frightening them into fleeing straight into it. We'll never know, but don't let the water touch you. Strange things have happened to flesh when contacted. Use the handles on the vials." Seeing Talon looking dubious, he added, "Now you know why I need someone brave."

"Or foolish."

"Or that."

Talon noticed Noren smirking, while the swordsman sneered, the knight looked nauseated, and the woman grinned. The kryll yawned. Talon only trusted him and the knight, if anyone. And maybe the cat.

Viland strode around the grove's edge while the others trailed along, stopping between the trees and the wall. As they watched, the wizard stretched out both hands and spoke in tones that Talon recognized. The trees began to lean sideways as a whorl of darkness filled the space between them; birds squawked furiously as they fled into the night sky. The mynx growled low in its throat and Noren said nothing to calm it, the lorenia lines on his face glowing bright blue at the magic afoot. Light seemed to disappear into the haphazardly shaped opening, as if the chaos beyond it hungered for the life out here. The Ever Gate looked nothing like a doorway, and its edges continued to ebb and flow as it became more substantial. Viland stopped speaking and dropped both arms to his sides.

"Quickly now," he said, gesturing toward it as the others began shuffling forward.

Talon cocked an eyebrow, realizing that he was ignorant of things that hadn't even occurred to him yet. "If you aren't coming with us, how do we open it to return?"

"A spell is only needed to open it from outside. The challenge of escaping is finding the door again. Noren will do that. Only karelia can find their way."

Talon gripped his sword harder, not caring for relying on a sorelia's sense of direction. All karelia are excellent navigators, thanks to the goddess of intuition who had been one of their creators. But sorelia are a corrupted version of the karelian species and there is no telling how they differ. Besides, the Ever Pathways distorted everything that went into them. "What about the cat? Does it know the way back?"

Noren smirked at him for the implication that he wouldn't survive, the blue lorenia glow reflecting in his unfriendly eyes. The sorelia turned to the Ever Gate and gazed intently as if he could see something in the blackness beyond it that the others could not. Without a word, he stepped into it with the mynx. Against his better judgment, Talon followed. As if reacting to some energy he couldn't see, the blond hair on his arms rose as he passed through, a brief wave of severe cold rushed over him, and an acrid smell accompanied a wave of nausea. His vision went black for an instant, but that only spurred him forward, his feet coming to rest on firm turf. He paused to look around, the others joining and moving past him as if already familiar with the experience.

The Ever Gate, still open, appeared more like a doorway from this side, roughly rectangular, an edge of shimmering blackness surrounding a window of lighter darkness. Around it and in every direction lay a landscape not unlike Llurien itself, save that a twilight without end seemed to permeate the air. Mustiness filled his nostrils. Turbulent, dark clouds swirled overhead. Stands of unfamiliar trees randomly grew atop rolling hills and flat land alike, a thick forest standing some miles to one side, with steep mountain peaks farther beyond. Nearer trees blocked other views.

Noren and the mynx advanced in parallel toward the mountains with purpose. The lorenia lines on the sorelia's face were dimmer now, which surprised Talon, for he thought this land was so magical that the karelia's senses would've been almost overloaded here.

Talon's gaze fell on the young knight, whose chest plate bore the symbol of his rank—a sword crossed with a shield. He was a Knight of the Sword, the first rank out of training. That the shield icon had a halo around it surprised Talon, for while all knighthood rank symbols included the shield, if it was depicted glowing, that meant he had already earned the prestigious Knight of Coiryn honor for bravery. And yet he scanned their surroundings with troubled, fearful eyes. Talon glanced about once more only to discover that the Ever Gate had seemingly vanished. The mountains now ran behind them, too.

Seeing his startled reaction, the knight remarked, "It is of no use. *We* were lost within twenty paces. Only the sorelia can lead us out. Protect him with your life, for your soul depends on it."

Talon nodded. What good were the senses if one could not trust them? Was it only his eyes that deceived him, or would his ears, too? The worst aspect of the disorientation was that he felt certain he was not, in fact, disoriented. He asked, "Why is a Knight of Coiryn working for a wizard?"

The knight frowned, scratching at two days of black stubble. "I must repay a debt, and no other reason. The name is Dal."

"Talon. A debt for what?"

"My own affair."

"Fair enough. You've been here before?"

"Once."

"And how many times until your debt is paid?"

"I do not know."

Talon stifled a grunt. No man should enter into a bargain without knowing the terms. "The knighthood doesn't know, I assume."

Dal glanced suspiciously at him but then relaxed. "It'd be my head or my honor."

"One as good as the other," commented Talon, though he didn't agree. But he knew knights believed that and wanted at least one person on his side while in this place. The knight gave him an appraising look. Talon asked, "What does Viland do with this silver elixir?"

"That I do not know, nor do I wish to."

"What if he's doing something the knighthood would disapprove of?"

The knight smirked. "Now you know why I don't ask."

Talon stifled a frown. "Ignorance won't save you from a Solon Judge's sentence should the truth be awful."

Dal sighed. "I know, but I have no choice in the matter and would rather not know. Sleep is hard to come by as it is."

Talon wondered what kept the man awake at night. Was it his conscience? He knew better than to ask personal details and instead inquired, "What can you tell me about this place?"

"Be on your guard. And there is no shame in running from that which cannot be predicted, in behavior or otherwise." Despite his words, an expression of great bitterness swept over Dal's rugged features.

Talon suspected that this admission of fleeing bothered him. "Have you fought anything here?"

"No."

"Run from anything?"

This time a spark of anger lit Dal's eyes and he appeared to choose his words carefully. "A Knight of Coiryn does not run from anything lightly, you can be sure of that."

"I am. What did you run from?"

"Pray to Coiryn you don't find out."

Sensing an end to their talk, Talon wondered if the god of courage, or any of the other gods, held dominion in this place. Had they created it along with Llurien? It seemed likely, as his world and Everland were connected, but for what purpose? Maybe the gods used it to travel, but from what Talon knew, they could appear anywhere in an instant, so why would they need the paths?

Maybe the City of the Gods lay here. That would explain why getting lost was so easy, for it was said that the gods didn't want visitors; if they wanted you, they'd appear before you. Or you'd suddenly appear before *them*.

Seeing the woman admiring him from the corner of her dark, mysterious eyes, Talon moved closer. "Why are you here?"

"Enchanting my blades," she said, gripping the twin swords in their scabbards. Her curious gaze held his without flinching and he decided he liked her.

"Cold steel is all you need."

Talon's mother had been a valend wizard—one who creates magic items for a living—but his knight father had instilled in him the value of not relying on anything but skill to win the day. This swordswoman cut a fine figure in the black leather. Many a man had likely been nicked by one of her blades for an improper advance, but he felt undeterred.

She replied, "An advantage gained is an advantage earned."

He nodded. "How will you do it?"

"Dip them in the Poison Pond. The silver elixir will give them powers."

"Powers you can't control," he observed. "Chaos Blades, they're called in the stories. It is foolish."

She laughed, the sound taking an eerie tone in this disturbed land, and her mirth quickly vanished on hearing it. "It will be foolish for anyone to cross blades with me again! The chaos will be theirs to fear, not mine."

"So you hope."

"And what of you?" the woman asked, eyeing his muscled physique so intently that the other swordsman, who'd been observing them, scowled darkly. "Are you just a thief, or is there more to you?"

He smiled. "When I unsheathe my sword, you'll have your answer."

"Jenar Darkfire isn't the only one who wishes to know this," observed the kryll, falling in beside them, his smooth gait at once suggestive of relaxed ease and great might, as if the latter caused the former. Like many kryll, he gave the impression of being unconcerned by the prospect of danger—their legendary mastery of weapons was no doubt one reason for this. His leather armor differed little from Talon's except in style and brown color. Kryll were acrobatic and preferred nimbleness to the encumbrance of heavier armor. Besides, why be struck and trust your armor to save you when you can avoid the blow altogether? He had a strong brow and straight nose typical of the species, black hair in a tight braid, red eyes regarding Talon calmly.

"Who are you, Talon the Nyborian?" the kryll asked.

Talon shrugged, noting that the kryll was as tall as he and almost as muscular, though slimmer and more refined, his agility easily apparent in the smooth walk. Talon had little interest in relating his past, for it didn't matter. "I'm a man with a sword."

Appraising him, the kryll asked, "Trained by kryll?"

"My father. A knight."

"To become one? And yet you are not."

Hearing a question he would rather not answer, Talon asked, "What brings you here?"

"I come for the elixir as well, to study it." He nodded his head as if bowing. "Mikolyn of House Rivermoon."

Talon nodded his understanding. Every kryll has a subject to which he devotes considerable research, becoming an expert. "Then you're not here to study men with swords."

Mikolyn laughed. "Indeed. May your blade fly as true as your wit, Stormbringer. We shall have need of both ere long."

"You couldn't find silver elixir on Llurien? Someone must have it."

"It is illegal to possess in most places. And those with it do not admit to it, or part with it lightly, since it is so hard to acquire. Besides, how can I truly understand it if I have not seen its source?"

"There wasn't anything less dangerous to study?"

Mikolyn smiled. "How am I to make a name for myself studying things as ordinary as men with swords?"

Talon appreciated a turn of phrase but remarked, "Everyone here wants attention. I want to avoid it."

"Perhaps you should change your name. It is rather striking."

"What makes you think I haven't already?"

The kryll smiled. "We must share a drink of kryllan wine upon our return, you and I. Perhaps there's much to learn from you after all."

Talon was about to respond when his ears caught a dull thudding that he recognized as hooves, but there was something strangely heavy about the sound. It seemed like a single horse but somehow not, but then far away sounds traveled differently here, seeming muted or coming from the wrong direction instead of from the source. A glance at the kryll and Noren showed that they were aware of it, too. So was the mynx, its ears up. The noise grew louder and the sorelia gestured to a crop of bushes that they hurried to get behind.

Staring toward the source, Talon sensed something unnatural when two dozen horses crested a hill at a gallop and charged toward them. Black to the last, they moved in four rows of six, tightly bunched, like a military formation. Nothing could explain that, unless invisible riders were guiding them. They turned to one side in unison, then turned again moments later.

"They're moving together," Talon observed, "hooves landing as one."

"That's just wrong," muttered the knight in distaste.

"The Ever Fiend is controlling them," Noren explained with certainty, causing the woman to murmur in concern.

"He's searching for us?" Jenar asked, looking around nervously.

"Not us specifically," the sorelia replied, and the others seemed to relax.

"How do you know this?" Talon asked. That Talon knew nothing of this land except stories from his youth made him feel uncomfortably unprepared.

"Do you have a better explanation?"

Talon had to admit he did not. Part of him still did not accept that this children's bogeyman existed, even though other things about this realm were confirmed. The horde of horses wheeled away, disappearing over another rise until the sound of their hooves faded away and the group could carry on.

The Nyborian found the swordsman striding beside him, chainmail-covered chest puffed up. A thin black mustache seemed designed to bolster his manliness while the cocky gaze had the opposite effect of making him seem weak. "The man you replaced is dead," Orin said, amused, "in case you were wondering."

Talon had already sized up this fellow and asked, "Your doing?"

The man snorted. "No. Why? Worried I'll stick my sword in you?"

"Only if I turn my back."

Jenar laughed and Orin turned red. "Shut your mouth, Jenar!"

"So what happened to your friend?" Talon asked, hiding his amusement.

"Wasn't my friend, but maybe you'll run into him here and he'll tell you."

"You said he's dead."

For an answer, Orin grinned and boasted, "Been here three times already. Doubt you'll last that long."

"If I have to do it with you, certainly not."

Jenar laughed again and Orin angrily retorted, "None of my friends are brave enough to come."

Talon observed. "Or foolish enough. You come for vanity?"

Orin scowled as if to deny it and then glared. "Don't act like you're better than me, Stormbringer. You got caught stealing to earn your place here."

"Same as you? I don't see you getting past a jhaikan, mynx, or riven."

"I could if I wanted to! Didn't need to."

"Then how did you earn your place?"

When Orin didn't answer, Noren remarked over one shoulder, "He has inclinations Viland helps him satisfy, in exchange for his aid."

Talon cocked an eyebrow. He didn't really want to know, didn't care, and decided their conversation was over. The man's demeanor stifled Talon's temptation to ask if he knew what Viland did with the elixir, for he would likely get a boastful answer that wasn't well informed. The sorelia was far likelier to know, though perhaps unwilling to tell. Talon quickened his pace slightly and soon fell in beside Noren and the mynx, who strode casually, suggesting no danger neared them just now.

The sorelia looked at him shrewdly. "You have gray eyes, Nyborian."

Talon sensed the sorelia was suggesting something. Those damn karelia saw too many things. "What of it?"

"You have a karelian ancestor."

He failed to hide a surprised reaction that Noren had figured that out. He had learned on the streets that eyes can betray a man, just not in this particular way. Someone on his mother's side had been karelian. "How you can tell that?"

"Humans are most often brown-eyed. Most karelia are green. Gray eyes can appear to be green and in a human it's one indication of a potential karelian ancestor."

"*Potential,*" Talon stressed. "The Iris Myth is kerr shit."

Each of the seven groups of gods associates itself with a color in the spectrum, and since each group created a species, their species usually has that color eyes. The traits of the gods also dominate that species' outlook. Since all seven groups created humans together, mixing their traits, the colors mixed, too, causing most humans to have brown eyes—and a temperament far more variable than any other species. Since humans are forever trying to decide what each other is really like, and often resort to superficial means of assessing another human's character, the Iris Myth was born. Any human without brown eyes is thought to have another species as an ancestor, and since each species is associated with certain character traits, that suggests which traits dominate the human, too.

Talon added, "Gray eyes can also appear blue, which would suggest I had a jhaikan ancestor instead. Boys used to taunt me with that, but no one ever said it to me twice."

Noren grinned. "Why? Did you assault them?

"Something like that," he admitted.

"Do you see nothing amusing about this, considering the gods of wrath, cruelty, cunning, and domination created jhaikan?"

Behind them, Olin snorted.

Noren continued, "If it's wrong, then why do most karelia have green eyes like the four gods who created them? Or jhaikan blue like their gods?"

"My gray eyes don't mean I have a jhaikan ancestor, any more than your blue eyes do."

"We sorelia are an accident of mischief, and so our irises are more random in color, like you humans."

"*Random*," Talon stressed.

Noren smiled at Talon without friendliness. "Do your eyes see things other humans don't?"

"No," he lied, then changed the subject. "You seem in league with this wizard. What does he do with this elixir?"

"You must get it regardless, Stormbringer."

Talon sensed the sorelia understood his intent to refuse this quest depending on what he learned. Those damn karelia were too smart sometimes. He decided not to pretend that Noren was wrong, and replied, "I prefer a clear conscience."

"Strange, for a thief."

He let that pass. "You're avoiding the question."

"You can ask him yourself."

"He's unlikely to tell me."

"And you think I'm more likely?"

"No, it's just that you're with me at the moment. Is the answer so terrible that you fear to tell, or are you afraid of what I'll do with the knowledge?"

Noren smiled. "No on both counts. I fear little, and certainly not just a man with a sword, however impressive he may appear. And what could you do? Viland is respected. You are not."

Apparently sorelia lacked karelian tact, but Talon wasn't one for hurt feelings. He sensed no answers were coming and decided to ask the wizard before handing over the vials. He changed the subject again. "What do you gain from all this?"

"Access to this land. Unguarded Ever Gates are hard to find."

Wondering how awful the answer would be, Talon asked, "What does a sorelia want here?"

Noren gave his first unreserved smile. "Nyborian, where some see horrors, others see treasures unimaginable, and that is what I've come for. I have the same deal with the wizard as you. I keep whatever I find, and since the pathways keep changing, the path I tread is never the same twice. It always brings me something new, no matter how many times I walk it."

"And how many times is that?" For an answer, Talon received only a smile. "What do you do with the things you find?"

Noren looked away with a smirk. "Sell or give them to the unsuspecting. Weapons are seldom fun for that, as they don't inflict something on the wielder. But anything that can be worn, like magical armor, is typically cursed. And the wearer often cannot remove it."

Talon glowered. This sorelia was the evil one, it seemed, not the wizard. Or maybe Noren was just worse. Stopping him from returning cursed items might be more important than returning without the elixir. "Why do this to people? For the sake of evil?"

"Perhaps. Maybe I have a different sense of justice than you."

"Undoubtedly. How is it justice to sell cursed items to unsuspecting people?"

"Those who seek an advantage over others through magic ought to pay the price for their ambition."

Thinking of Jenar, Talon glanced back to see her scowling intensely at the sorelia, who seemed to know it as if he had eyes in the back of his head, for the way he grinned. "What of your wizard?" Talon asked. "He seeks advantage through this elixir."

"He will destroy himself sooner or later, probably with it."

"You care nothing for him."

"I'm sorelian. And he is not a friend, just a business partner. I'm sure you understand."

Talon did indeed and hadn't expected much more. "You've kept nothing you've found here? Not even one thing?"

"I never said that."

"What was it?"

The karelia gazed at him as if trying to decide how much impact a revelation could have. "The sword," Noren admitted, hand on the hilt.

"What does it do?"

"Pray you never find out from me swinging it at you."

Normally Talon ignored such warnings, but a Chaos Blade was not something to face knowingly. If the stories were true, one didn't have to strike you to wreak havoc of unnatural kinds.

The group continued in silence, scanning for trouble as they skirted forests at a distance. Woods offered a place to hide but might be the place from where a threat emerged. Even the plants were a danger. They moved as if controlled by a mind. One tree held a humanoid skeleton it seemed to be playing with. An entire grove briefly marched along the horizon like a herd of animals before disappearing toward some unseen goal.

Some grass fields they trod had clearly been grazed by something, while others were tall and showed signs of recent passage by someone. In one instance, Noren indicated the tracks were their own; they had not lost their way, but the landscape had shifted as if sections of land floated like islands on an unseen sea. Even distinctive mountains changed location, suggesting that the land masses rotated, too.

Talon couldn't understand how Noren knew where they were going. When asked, the sorelia admitted that his gods-given sixth sense allowed him to feel where the Poison Pond was, no matter what happened. It explained why he sometimes changed direction abruptly. Though a sorelia couldn't be trusted, they had no choice but to do so. The feeling of vulnerability that this introduced rankled Talon.

That feeling worsened when they reached an uncovered, dark stone bridge that spanned a river of black water a hundred yards wide. Three boats with paddles were moored to each side and, a short distance away, the waters emptied into a wide expanse that Noren called the Lake of Souls. Talon, Noren, and the mynx took the lead, with Dal and Mikolyn on rear guard while Jenar and Orin took the middle. The span showed signs of being ancient and unfamiliar in some way Talon couldn't place. The low walls had crumbled in places, archaic words and symbols appearing there at even intervals, some resembling magic words and others indecipherable.

"What do the words say?" the knight asked, booted feet thudding on the bridge.

"Don't read them aloud," cautioned Noren, eyes stern.

"Why?" Talon asked, curious what would happen but not interested in finding out the hard way. He supposed that he did trust the sorelia with certain things.

"If you have talent for magic," Noren replied, "there's no telling what might happen."

Mockingly, Jenar said, "Then I guess I shouldn't read them."

Talon arched an eyebrow. "You have the gift?"

"If you want to call it that. Never cared for the studying, so talent is all I have. No skill."

Noren eyed her dismissively. "You come here for power and yet refuse to master that which you were born with. Fool."

She bristled until Talon laid a hand on her arm. "Ignore him. I know some of these words but not the others."

Jenar asked, "You have the talent, too?"

He nodded. Like most people with the gift of magic, he knew valenders—beginner spells to help get by in life and which generally acted on objects, not people. He didn't use them often, but some had proven invaluable more than once. "I prefer the sword."

"Another fool." Noren looked about to say more when the mynx's ears shot forward and the cat put both front paws on a wall to raise himself higher. He stared intently in the direction they were going and growled low. "Jhaikan," Noren announced, as if recognizing the cat's tone. Talon knew the cats were trained to give different vocalizations. "Quickly, we must hide."

CHAPTER THREE

THE SHADOW RIDERS

Talon drew his kryllan sword. "We'll engage here. The bridge is only wide enough for three to fight, which favors us." They might not get off in time to hide, which he didn't care much for anyway.

"There." Mikolyn pointed to half a dozen figures that emerged from behind a copse, running in their direction. He began swinging his nine-foot staff of Siaran oak in a twirling blur, the foot-long, steel endcaps whistling as his hands expertly moved between three leather-wrapped grips spaced inches apart. The jhaikan-staff resembled normal quarterstaffs with two exceptions—it could be dismantled into smaller pieces for travel and then reassembled, and, with a spoken word, the wielder could make blades protrude from either end like a spear or scythe. Mikolyn did this now to one end, giving himself slicing death there and bludgeoning power on the other side.

They outnumbered the jhaikan by one due to the battle mynx. A lone jhaikan could easily kill a half dozen normal opponents like Jenar or Orin, but with himself, a kryll, the mynx, and Noren, they stood a good chance. After a glance back, as if searching for a hiding place, Noren seemed to agree, issuing a command to the cat, who moved ahead of them to stand guard.

Talon strode to the bridge's apex and motioned for the kryll and sorelia to flank him, which they did. The knight grumbled that he should take Talon's place, but the Nyborian's commanding demeanor silenced him. Dal pulled a long sword from a scabbard and stood between Jenar, her twin swords ready, and the worried-looking Orin.

"Is there anything supernatural about these jhaikan?" Talon asked, looking at Noren to see if the lorenia lines on his face were lighting up. But then they could react to anything of that sort, and onlookers had no way of knowing what a karelia was sensing.

"Not that I see." As Noren spoke, he unsheathed a karelian longsword, the blade evenly curved with a single cutting edge. A soft green light shone around the black metal and in the magic lettering on the blade, the emerald alight in the pommel beneath his small hands.

Talon remarked, "You must not fight in the dark much, carrying a glowing sword like that."

Noren smirked. "I thought you said your eyes don't see things others can't."

Talon didn't respond, as all time for chatter ended when the six jhaikan reached the bridge at a run. Each stood over nine feet and moved fast on two powerful legs, their clawed hands empty. Sinuous tails swayed with agitation behind them, the spike on the end a formidable weapon. From their wide mouths, rows of serrated teeth were another danger. Their keen sense of smell in a snout-like muzzle could help them hone in on someone, but instead they seemed intent on listening intensely, their ears rapidly swiveling independently of each other.

Their reptilian skin changed colors haphazardly, as if they'd lost all control of their camouflaging abilities. They often glanced backward as they approached, an uncommon sight for a violent species known for stalking and hunting prey. Their obvious flight was a powerful sight, for jhaikan were the thing from which all others on Llurien fled. That disturbed Talon more than the sight of each of them wearing plate armor, for the species normally eschewed such protection, opting for just forearm bracers and mailed gloves with the fingertips removed.

But worst of all was the damage that armor had taken. There were gashes from swords that might've been afire for the scorch marks left behind. White frost covered dents. And wiggling arrows seemed to be trying to bore their way deeper. Talon sensed their numbers were reduced and wondered if challenging the leader to single combat would earn them safe passage if he emerged victorious, as that was the jhaikan custom.

"Should we challenge them?" he asked of Mikolyn. Kryll were traditional enemies of jhaikan, more so than any other species, and read their moods better, which became easier as their foe advanced up the bridge, their haste even more apparent.

"No," answered Orin a little too emphatically.

Mikolyn seemed to agree. "They may not acknowledge. Something is amiss among them."

Talon nodded, sensing the same. Jhaikan were masters of strategy, but he felt certain they just wanted to get past them. Maybe he and the others should've just stepped aside, but now it was too late. With a snarl, the center jhaikan ignored the mynx, who leapt at one of the others, and came straight for Talon.

A steel-gloved hand swung for his sword as if to grasp it, but instead of blocking, Talon turned his weapon's point so the other's hand would impale itself. The jhaikan's glove prevented penetration and its other clawed hand flew toward him. Talon ducked and slashed at its forward leg, the blade coming away red. The jhaikan feigned another swing but Talon sensed the intent and severed the limb. His jhaikan howled and Talon stabbed it through the chest before decapitating it with one tremendous blow.

He stole a glance at the others. Noren seemed unable to get past his mynx, who swiped low at another jhaikan, which had bites and claw wounds to both legs and arms. The cat's armor had been dented in two places. Mikolyn's jhaikan had one arm hanging uselessly but the kryll had been slashed across the chest. He seemed unaffected, jhaikan-staff still whistling through the air, this time crushing the jhaikan's collarbone. The remaining jhaikan hanging back seemed ready to charge when not looking nervously over their shoulders. Talon risked a look but couldn't see what they were so afraid of.

The mynx clamped down on a jhaikan's arm, which the jhaikan raised high, exposing the cat's unprotected belly. Talon leapt forward and sliced off the limb, the jhaikan roaring in fury but unable to stop Talon's sword from cutting its torso nearly in half. At the same moment, Mikolyn let out a battle cry and smashed his opponent's skull in so hard that the jhaikan tumbled over the bridge's low wall. A splash below led to a sickening sizzling sound so odd that both kryll and Nyborian looked over the edge to see what was happening. The body turned red as if boiling, the water around it seething with bubbles, before it sank.

Seeing the way clearer, the remaining three jhaikan charged. Noren stepped aside, as did Jenar and Orin, but Dal stood his ground, swinging hard at the lead jhaikan, who blocked the blow and slashed his chest so hard that it flung him onto his back. The three jhaikan ran straight over him and away, soon disappearing.

Talon helped the knight up, noticing that his destroyed breastplate hung poorly, the straps holding it on partially severed. With a yank, he pulled it off and tossed it aside.

"We need to get off this bridge before whatever they're running from gets here."

"It must be fearsome," observed the kryll, wincing in pain. "We would've had a worse time had they not been so determined to get past us."

Noren spent a moment tending to his mynx and saying words in sorelian that Talon didn't recognize. He turned to Talon. "My cat's name," he began, "is Nightwish. Should you desire it, he will follow your commands from here onward."

"Why?"

"You saved his life. I've seen to it that he will obey you."

Talon wondered if any trickery was afoot, but the sorelia seemed genuine. Did he have a sense of honor after all? Talon hadn't expected that. But he couldn't trust someone who wanted to loose cursed items on the unsuspecting. The cat, being an animal, wouldn't have duplicity, so perhaps the beast could be trusted. Talon would take care not to do the same with the sorelia.

The sound of horses galloping stopped further conversation. Talon motioned for everyone to run back the way they'd come. The rowboats beside the bridge offered the only hiding place. Talon lifted one from the black water and flipped it over as Dal and the swordsman took another and everyone crawled under, careful not to let the oozing liquid dripping from the bottoms touch them. No sooner had they gotten out of sight than a nightmare came into view.

The two dozen horses they'd seen earlier crested a hill in apparent pursuit of the jhaikan, heading straight for the bridge. Like before, they moved in unison and in formation, but this time, they bore visible riders, all shimmering blackness like shadows that rippled, glowing armor and weapons further masking their forms. Their dress and the curved blades in their hands reminded Talon of Coiryn Riders, but the god of courage they were named after would've been appalled by this sight. Talon repositioned himself to peer out from under the curved edge of the upside down rowboat, unable to determine what species the riders resembled, had they ever existed in flesh and blood. One held a lance upright, a black-and-white pennant flying from it, the symbol hard to see.

The hooves struck the stone bridge with a clatter that slowed as the riders neared and finally stopped, to Talon's dismay. Had the dead jhaikan been thrown into the river, the ghostly riders might've continued, but he couldn't blame them for investigating the corpses at their feet. He would have done the same. How often did they run across fresh bodies in this cursed place? That someone had done it meant they'd be on the lookout for the culprits. Talon and the others would not remain undetected for long.

Two riders dismounted and walked among the jhaikan bodies. Through the cold breath escaping their mouths, Talon saw their lips move. At the same moment, an eerie breeze seemed to stir up. But then he realized the wind was carrying words, and the breeze he felt was actually their voices slithering through the air. Chills raced down his spine. That he couldn't understand what was said seemed a blessing.

"They're trying to raise the jhaikan," whispered Noren beside him.

"Perfect," Talon replied. "Undead jhaikan is just what this place needs."

"Quiet! Both of you!" Jenar fiercely whispered.

A rider turned in their direction but returned his gaze to the dead before him. With a groan, two jhaikan slowly rose, one missing an arm and the other its head, and soon they entered into unholy conversation with their new masters, who sent them shuffling down the bridge toward Talon and the others. On reaching the end, they headed straight toward Talon's hiding place.

"Be ready," the Nyborian whispered, gripping his sword.

"By the gods," Jenar said, eyes wide.

Talon laid a hand on her, feeling protective. The undead jhaikan came perilously close, but from their gait he sensed they'd pass by. And they did, following the river. Meanwhile, the mounted horsemen dashed from the bridge with a racket that included the blowing of a horn, its clarion call dissonant and grating in the surreal atmosphere. If the horn had any effect, he couldn't tell. Staying behind were the two dismounted riders and their black horses, for what purpose Talon couldn't tell, but they seemed intent on remaining.

"Now we can be worried," he remarked.

"Indeed," whispered Noren. "Fortunately, those with the horn have left, or else we'd emerge only to have them all return, for I suspect it is used to call other riders to them."

Talon observed, "My blade is not magical."

The sorelia nodded. "Only mine is, so this fight will be mine. It is unlikely that normal weapons will hurt them. You and Nightwish will come. They will not know that only I am a danger to them."

Talon understood his role but hoped the sorelia wasn't being overconfident. "Surprise is impossible. We must get to the bridge before they can mount and ride past us."

"What if they ride the other way?" Jenar whispered.

He looked back at her silently, his flat gaze indicating that wouldn't be good. He said to Noren, "Nightwish should run to the bridge. He'll get there faster than either of us."

"Are you sure this is a good idea?" the knight whispered from the other rowboat.

Talon shook his head. "Follow, but do not get in the way of the charge."

"Agreed."

With a final look at the sorelia, who nodded consent, Talon thrust the rowboat up and off. The two riders whirled in their direction as Nightwish sprinted toward them, the Nyborian and Noren close behind, Jenar taking her time to follow. The other rowboat lifted up hastily as the kryll and knight emerged and followed them, Orin bringing up the rear.

Just as Talon feared, the riders mounted their horses to drive toward them, but the mynx was faster, reaching the bridge's end just as the first rider tried to jump past. The cat leapt at steed and rider, bearing both to the ground with a growl and then springing free. Still running, Talon pulled a dagger from his waist and hurled it at the fallen rider, who rose with surprising speed and swung a flaming sword at Nightwish. Despite hitting point first, Talon's blade bounced harmlessly away but distracted the rider, who missed the mynx. The cat jumped free and pounced on the fallen horse, which was trying to rise but now found a battle-trained mynx clawing its throat out.

Talon saw that the second rider would get by them, but suddenly a spear flew past his head from behind and impaled the horse, which staggered and fell to its front knees, throwing its rider to the ground. Talon leapt at the horse and sliced deep through its neck even as the beast fell dead, felled by what Talon only new realized was Mikolyn's jhaikan-staff.

In an instant, its rider was on him, swinging a frost-rimed flail. Talon ducked and the spiked ball flew past his head before circling again at a lower arc. The flail's chain wrapped around his upraised sword, yanking it from his suddenly frost-covered hand, but now the rider's weapon was useless until Talon's blade was removed from the ball and chain.

Talon glanced at Noren, whose black sword, glowing green, clashed with his opponent's flaming steel. Despite being shorter by a foot, the sorelia easily held his own and began pressing the rider backward before plunging the sword into its chest. Clutching Noren's blade with both black hands, the rider screamed as the black blade burst into green fire. The rider crumbled to dust, the flames on its dropped sword extinguishing.

"Talon! Here!" Jenar yelled.

He turned to see one of her swords flying through the air. With a quick roll toward it, he caught the hilt and turned, just in time to see his opponent throw a knife that he narrowly dodged. A grunt of pain behind sounded like Mikolyn and Talon suspected the kryll had been hit by it. He engaged the shadowy rider, luring it away from Noren, who quietly approached it from behind. The sorelia stabbed the glowing blade through the rider's back with the same results as on the previous opponent. Noren promptly scooped the ashes into a pouch before returning to the other pile to do the same. Talon didn't want to know what he intended to do with the ashes.

"We don't have time for souvenirs," he said, retrieving his sword and returning Jenar's. As their eyes met, another thing they didn't have time for came to mind. Though she hadn't participated in the battle much, Jenar looked invigorated and excited, lips parted, eyes alight. A sudden desire to kiss those lips surprised him with its strength, but he settled for an intense look of gratitude that made her blush and look away.

The sorelia didn't respond to Talon but took both the riders' weapons. He pulled a folded sack from within his armor and dropped them in, then slung it over one shoulder. "We must go, and quickly. The others are bound to return."

"Noren," the knight called from where he stood beside Mikolyn, who held one red hand to his side, a bloody dagger at his feet. "A potion healed his chest but had no effect on this new wound."

The sorelia approached and looked at the dagger that had caused the wound. "A Chaos Blade. The wound will not heal here."

"What can we do?"

Noren shrugged. "Magic is unpredictable until we're back on Llurien. The wound doesn't appear serious."

Mikolyn nodded grimly and pulled a bandage from a pouch at his waist, binding the wound as he could. As the others prepared to leave, Talon noticed Jenar pick up the Chaos Dagger and put it in her belt. He noticed Orin hanging back and stifled a frown, for Orin had made no secret of being willing to let others do the fighting while he kept himself safe. The swordsman was a liability and might get them killed if depended on.

Talon went to the rowboats and shoved two into the black water to suggest to anyone who came looking for them that they'd headed downriver toward the Lake of Souls.

As they crossed the bridge and continued on the other side, Dal remarked, "Those riders were from Avalends."

Talon nodded, having also recognized their tunic's insignia of a castle astride a river. The city lay to the east of Nybor beyond the plains of Lorne. Not expecting an answer, he asked, "What are they doing here?"

Noren pursed his lips. "Those were the Royal Riders of Avalends, I suspect. They haven't been seen in hundreds of years, since they entered Everland in search of their queen."

"The one who disappeared?" asked Talon, recalling the story from his schooling.

"Yes. She was kidnapped and thought to have been brought here by jhaikan, so the riders followed."

Jenar asked, "Why would they have brought her here?"

"They wouldn't have, and didn't."

"Then what happened to her?"

Noren grinned. "They ate her.

CHAPTER FOUR

THE POISON POND

A quarter hour later, Talon still felt that there was too much risk of the other Shadow Riders finding them. At his suggestion, they'd followed the riders' trail through swaying, tall grass in the hope of not leaving behind a trail of their own. To one side rolled hills. A vast plain stretched away on the other. Ahead lay a thick forest that seemed like a bad idea to enter.

"Do we intend to go in?" Talon asked Noren.

The sorelia shook his head. "We are near. I anticipate the scenery changing before we reach the woods, and being more like what surrounds the pond."

"How can you expect that?"

Noren eyed him, as if considering. "Do you not feel it? Search your senses."

"For what?"

"A sense of foreboding more acute than the rest, and in a specific direction from where you're facing. Once aware of it, you can feel its strength ebb and flow with your proximity to the source."

Behind them, Orin grunted. "And you karelia walk *toward* these things."

"Who else but us? Certainly not the likes of you." Noren paid no attention to the scowl his words caused.

Mikolyn let out a gasp and leaned hard on his jhaikanstaff for support. The others gathered around as Talon pulled the kryll's hand from his wound, noticing the frigid skin. The knife wound had turned black, tinged with blue frost that seemed to be encroaching from the edges as if working its way deeper.

"What is it?" Mikolyn asked, straining to see. "What's happening?"

Noren shook his head. "You're infected."

"With what?" Talon asked.

The sorelia shrugged. "If we do not hurry and get him back to Llurien, we shall find out."

"Then we return now," urged Talon, putting one of the kryll's arms around his shoulders and turning back toward the trail through the grass.

"No," disagreed Noren. "We are too close. It will take a short time to complete our task."

"You can't do it without me," Talon bluffed, for he saw no reason why the others couldn't get the silver elixir, unless something about this Poison Pond was so terrifying that the others wouldn't approach and he would. Certainly the kryll had the courage, but now this was a moot point. Perhaps he was the only one. The sorelia had admitted, when asked, that he needed to suppress supernatural life forms near the pond while Talon collected the prize, or else he would have done it himself.

"And you cannot return without me," Noren answered.

"You just told me how."

"No, I told you how to sense the Poison Pond, not an Ever Gate, much less the right one, and I doubt if you have the capability either way."

"You said yourself that I have karelian blood."

"But not karelian refinement. You do not know the art, have not been trained, and any talent you have will be diluted by your human ancestry. Don't be a fool. You're wasting time. If you really want to save him, then continue with us."

Without waiting to see if Talon was following, the sorelia led Nightwish toward what had just been a green canopy of trees ahead but which was now rolling hills with sparse underbrush. The sight sobered Talon. Used to finding his way with the sun or stars, or knowledge of an area, with landmarks like mountains that weren't moving, he felt no hope of escaping this land without the cursed sorelia, who clearly had little respect for anyone's life.

"Do as he asks," said Mikolyn, watching everyone follow Noren, "for he is right."

With the kryll's arm still around his shoulders, Talon grimaced but said nothing as they joined the others, who glanced back with a mixture of relief and regret, as if afraid of what Mikolyn might turn into. If someone suggested leaving the kryll behind so they wouldn't be around to find out, Talon would run them through. He exchanged a few quiet words of support and thanks with Mikolyn, who professed to not wanting to be a burden, before realizing aloud that the big Nyborian showed no signs of being burdened at all.

Miles later, Noren motioned for everyone to stop and sent Nightwish scampering up a hill before them, the cat moving with its tail low as if spooked. It slunk near the crest of the hill and slowly inched forward, ears alert and head snapping back and forth quickly. With a flick of its tail, it inched backward and then finally rose and came trotting back.

"We are there?" Talon surmised, sensing something even before the mynx's actions.

The sorelia patted the cat's head. "Yes, and something is near the water, as suspected. You may draw your weapons if you feel comforted by doing so, but none of you have one that will help you, save the girl."

Jenar looked surprised until the karelia eyed the Chaos Dagger tucked into her waistband. Her cheeks turned red. "Maybe I should go to the pond and enchant my swords first. Then we'll have two more."

Noren replied, "You won't make it there alive, or sane anyway, if I do not becalm that which lurks here." He gazed at her silently, as if impressed. Then he turned to Talon. "Perhaps I don't need you after all. It seems we have one with the courage to do what you're here for."

The woman beamed and Orin snickered while Talon frowned. "What about the Shadow Riders' weapons?"

"Unless you brought a glove to handle them," the sorelia answered, "you're better off not touching one."

Talon couldn't argue that.

Noren led them around the hill, everyone alert. He didn't need to tell them to keep quiet, but Talon suspected that whatever was guarding the pond already knew they were here. The lorenia lines on the sorelia's face had been growing brighter, though that could've meant anything magical. Still, he sensed something menacing just out of sight and all around, an impression of invisible forces swirling in anticipation of a meal consisting of their souls. Nightwish's back was arched and the cat's fur stood on end.

Rounding the hill, they came upon the Poison Pond. Roughly oblong, it lay fifty yards across, half again as wide. The silver waters rippled from an unseen wind that didn't strike the onlookers, an occasional circle of waves spreading outward as if something under the surface had moved. The liquid was thick enough to obscure whatever lay beneath and radiated light that cast dancing shadows on several boulders near its edge. Jet black, knee-high reeds swayed at one end, rising from the pool. Across the way, two Asyander trees, their trunks stark white, stood rooted near the edge but leaned sharply away as if desperate to escape the water.

All around the pond were the footprints of animals, humanoid species, and other beings whose mark Talon couldn't identify for all his years of tracking in the wild. The area immediately before them had trampled grass as if it was the preferred area to consume the sinister toxin. Aside from plants, no other sign of life existed, and Talon had the distinct impression that only death awaited those who came here. He glanced at the others; all but Noren and Mikolyn had wide, staring eyes. The sorelia had been right—had Talon known the growing sense of foreboding that he had been feeling had come from here, he would have been able to follow it without error to its source, just as Noren had. The realization made his stomach knot. He couldn't help putting one hand on his sword hilt and looking over each shoulder warily.

As the sorelia began gesturing and whispering words of magic, some of which Talon recognized, the feeling of dread began to fade. Was the danger afraid of them now? Repulsed? Intimidated? Or just realizing that the conquest was not that easy after all? He felt glad for Noren's skills, as creepy as the karelian species could sometimes be. Sometimes having one with you proved a boon, but sorelia lacked the honor that karelia exuded.

"It is time," Noren said in Antarian, the language common to all. He continued moving his arms in a pattern as if tracing something in the air. Talon had the impression that as long as the sorelia did this, his spell remained in effect. "We will wait here, Stormbringer, while you retrieve the elixir. Be careful not to touch it. If you think the Shadow

Rider's dagger caused a nasty wound in that kryll, it is nothing compared to the elixir's touch."

Before he could set off, Jenar appeared beside him, one hand on his bicep. She was so close that the faint scent of lluvien perfume, which he had not noticed before, filled his nostrils. She seemed somehow smaller, her eyes wide and head tilted down despite being shorter than him.

"Talon," she whispered. She seemed intent on saying more but didn't, as if inhibited by fear.

"Stay here with the others," he said reassuringly, trying to appear more unfazed than he was. "Nightwish will protect you while I'm at the water's edge. It will only be a minute."

"Stay wary," she advised.

He gripped her hand and then turned away, brushing her from his mind with an effort.

Drawing and raising his sword because instinct demanded it, Talon crept across the short green grass, which seemed unnaturally lush. He wondered if the nearby waters somehow invigorated it despite their name. He felt and sensed spirits hovering at the edge of his consciousness as if trying to probe him, his skin prickling. What good was a sword here? His fingers itched for the Chaos Blade that Jenar wore, but he didn't look back.

Now just strides from the Poison Pond, Talon turned his attention more fully to it. He had been aware of a hissing sound growing louder, and it seemed to come from the water itself. If something lurked just under it, ready to spring for him, he would never know until it did so, but he liked to think that Noren or even Viland would've told him if that was the case. They could've killed him long before now if his death was all they wanted. But then, maybe death wasn't what happened to those who fell in.

At the water's edge, Talon slowly crouched to one knee, ready to jump back if needed. Without looking, he unfastened one vial from the sash and popped the cork into the grass, which grew right to the water's edge. If the pool ever shrank and expanded, there was no sign of it, unless it was now at its fullest. Talon turned his sword so the point faced the water, to impale anything leaping from within. With his other hand, he lowered the vial to the surface, his eyes finally dropping to the task so as to avoid dipping too far and touching the dreaded liquid.

The vial's edge slipped into the pond, the viscous silver elixir oozing into the opening with a hiss like steam. Soon the flow stopped and he slowly lifted the bottle out, seeing the liquid fall away from its sides, none of it remaining on the vial. Until now, Talon hadn't considered the need to wipe excess elixir from a vial's exterior, but the question was moot. The falling droplets struck the surface as if striking a solid, expanding outward in a splash mark before slowly sinking. Talon stood the vial on the ground, stoppered it tightly with one hand, and put it back in his sash. In due time, he had completed the other vials and returned to the still-gesturing Noren as quickly as he dared, never turning his back to the Poison Pond. Jenar looked noticeably more relaxed than before, but then nothing had happened to him.

"It is done."

"Not quite," said Jenar, drawing her swords. She advanced with more bravado than Talon, whether because he had been unmolested or because she was intent to get this over with. Striding quickly, she made it to the shoreline and slid both blades into the silver elixir. She held them there for a dozen heartbeats and Talon wondered if she thought the amount of time submerged would impact what became of the now enchanted blades. Finally, she lifted both out, holding them point down so any liquid would pour off, which it did in twin streams. With a nervous little laugh, she held the blades up, and only then could Talon see that both glowed silver, illuminated from within.

Talon was about to urge her to return when something echoed her laughter, but wickedly. The direction from which it came could not be easily determined, and as Talon scanned back and forth, even behind, he saw the others doing so, too. Nightwish had risen to all fours, his tail bushy with fright for the only time Talon had seen. Suddenly Noren let out a gasp and fell back, his hands no longer moving, and the Nyborian knew that whatever he had been doing to suppress the supernatural here was over.

"It is here," the sorelia said, lorenia lines blazing anew as he pointed.

Beyond Jenar and across the shimmering waters, a cowled, black-robed figure floated toward them, no feet or hands visible. Within the hood lay only darkness that seemed to pull any light inward as if to devour it. At its approach, a chorus of terrified shrieks erupted from a horde of invisible beings near the pond. Orin cried out in fear. Dal uttered a prayer to Coiryn for strength. Jenar visibly trembled, the swords in both her hands shaking, drawing Talon's eyes, for only her blades were likely to kill the nightmare before them. Maybe it wasn't too late to risk touching the Shadow Riders' weapons in Noren's bag.

On reaching the silver water, the Ever Fiend stopped, and no one moved for long, tense moments. Talon stared into the hood and found himself unable to look away until the Fiend leaned down over the water, invisible hands seeming to support itself. The fabric never touched the silver surface while the Ever Fiend drank from the Poison Pond, which hissed and popped as its lips touched the surface.

After all the sorelia's warnings not to touch the stuff, Talon hadn't expected this. Did the silver elixir nourish the Ever Fiend when the liquid could destroy all others, rotting their bodies or soul? As Talon watched, the silhouette of arms began to appear as if the water replenished the foul creature, making it more substantial. The forearms and then hands materialized in black laced with silver, like veins on charred flesh. A white glow lit the inside of the hood so that Talon wasn't looking forward to the Ever Fiend rising.

"Why is it doing this?" Talon asked Noren, who stood beside him.

"I do not know," came the reply. "I have not seen it before."

"You've seen nothing drink from the pond?"

"No. It is death."

"How do you know if you've never seen it happen?"

"A fair question, but that is usually what's reported on Llurien."

"Usually?"

"Yes. A few have gone mad instead, mostly magic-users, and some have disappeared shortly after."

"Gone where?"

"No one knows."

When the sickening sizzle stopped, the pond's surface never moving, the Fiend straightened and raised its head. Talon caught a brief glimpse of a face that seemed human, the skin black, white eyes gleaming intensely, before darkness was again all that filled the hood. In that instant, he recognized an expression of strain and horror, as if the Ever Fiend was no better than the other tortured beings in this cursed land, merely the most powerful of them.

As everyone stood frozen, wondering what would come next, the Fiend spread both black arms and gestured downward toward the damned pond. Moaning in fear or despair, dozens of creatures emerged from between the nearby trees and from behind hills and boulders. Representing every species and quite a few animals, they ranged from skeletons and undead with rotting flesh and tattered clothes to those that seemed in the prime of their life. Scores of spirits, having lurked here all the while, materialized and flowed between them, their translucent bodies no less horrific. Two startled Talon as they brushed past him from behind, a wave of cold chilling his skin. A handful of ghosts waited on this side of the waters, all the others having been repelled to the far side by Noren's magic.

All wore an enthralled expression of subservience as they bent and drank the silver elixir, which coated the lips and chins of those with bodies. They otherwise showed no immediate effect, save for one that fell forward into the water and stopped moving, as if instantly killed. The spirits, by contrast, glowed more brightly, starting at their heads and spreading downward. One rose and shrieked uncontrollably, darting this way and that before rushing madly over a hill and out of sight, its hideous screaming audible for long moments until finally fading away. The Ever Fiend's laughter erupted from the cowl, darker than the blackness from which it emerged. At the sound, an undead kryll straightened and then fell face first into the Poison Pond, where it stopped moving.

As one, all of them stopped drinking and rose. Talon braced himself for some sort of assault, though it might take a minute for the horde to reach them. The ghosts nearest them stood with backs turned as if ignoring them, the two closest being just ten strides from a terrified Jenar. He scanned for an advantageous battleground, eyes returning to Jenar's swords. Then the Ever Fiend raised its arms once more and spoke a thickly accented line of archaic sounding words, which sounded like nothing Talen had ever heard.

Involuntarily, Talon took a step toward the Poison Pond before he strained to resist and stopped moving. Orin strode past him toward the water. Mikolyn and the knight did so more slowly, each sounding agonized as if fighting the movement as the Nyborian did. Only Noren remained still, but Talon saw the blaze of blue light from his lorenia lines and the visible effort on the karelia's face. Nightwish growled deep and turned to face his master, using both front paws to force Noren to the ground and hold him there. At the water's edge, Jenar dropped both swords and fell to her knees, hands on the grass, head bowing to the surface.

"No!" she cried, voice strangled.

And then her lips touched the silver elixir, the now familiar sizzling sound of someone drinking it reaching Talon's ears.

"By the gods," he said, heart pounding in fear for her. He reached for his dagger, arms easier to control than his feet, which took another step forward. By now, Orin had joined Jenar, whimpering in terror and pleading for mercy but to no avail. He, too, began to drink, but no sooner had he started than his body began to shake violently before falling into the Poison Pond, motionless. Jenar continued to drink beside him.

Wanting to save Jenar before she met the same fate, Talon surrendered to the compulsion to walk, two quick steps giving him the momentum to hurl a dagger at the Ever Fiend. As it flew, he again stopped his forward progress, which took all his strength. Whether through arrogance or something else, his target made no attempt to dodge. The weapon struck it in the chest but vanished in a burst of flame. The Ever Fiend stood unaffected.

At the water, the knight dropped to his knees with a clatter of plate mail and leaned over. As he began to drink, Mikolyn joined him. The Ever Fiend's minions stood vigil in eerie silence.

"Talon!" Noren called from beneath the mynx, voice strained. "The Chaos Blade. It is our only chance."

The Nyborian didn't respond but eyed the dagger on Jenar's belt. Getting that close when struggling to control his body seemed unwise, but the sorelia was right. Either that would work or they'd all be dead. Or worse.

He let himself be pulled forward more quickly, tongue straining for a taste of the elixir like a parched man. One failure of will and he would be fervently drinking. The compulsion strengthened as he neared, the Ever Fiend's hood turning toward him. Did it enjoy the challenge Talon posed? Did it consider him a strong member for its legions of the damned?

Talon reached Jenar's side and began to crouch, aware that he might not get up if either knee struck the ground. The sinister dagger hung within easy reach and he seized it and straightened, the move taking all his leg strength. With a twist of desperation, he wrenched his arm back and then hurled the dagger. The motion caused him to fall to both hands and knees, his head bowing to the dreadful liquid beside Jenar. He strained to lift his head and see the dagger's flight. Like before, the Ever Fiend didn't move, apparently unaware that this blade had advantages over the last. This time, when the blade struck, it sank deep into its heart. Talon heard a gasp from not only the Fiend, but also every other creature on the shore. Then, as one, they shrieked.

CHAPTER FIVE

A New Talent

Suddenly freed from the compulsion he had strained against, Talon nearly fell onto his backside in surprise. Across the silvery waters, the Ever Fiend writhed in agony, both black hands clutching at the dagger in its heart. A flash of white light lit the inside of the hood before darkness consumed it and the foul thing fell, head first, into the silver elixir, its upper body in the water. Each of its minions collapsed, as if dead. The ghosts vanished or fled. And Talon's companions lifted themselves up from the Poison Pond.

Talon grabbed Jenar by the shoulders and turned her to him. Her pupils had gone silver, like the elixir that ran down her chin from her drenched lips, a spot of it on her nose. She stared wide-eyed for a moment before scampering away and then sitting down, gasping. Talon leaned over Orin and ripped a rag from his tunic, then wiped Jenar's face with it. As he did so, the color of her eyes slowly returned to normal. Behind him, the knight and kryll were spitting, gagging, and cleaning themselves up. The cat had released its protective hold on its master Noren, who now approached them.

"Everyone come to me," the sorelia said, "quickly. I need to examine you."

"What for?" Jenar croaked, her breathing frantic, her knees pulled to her chest as if hugging them. "We are dead."

"Not yet," he replied. "You'd be face down if you were dead."

Taking the hint, Talon pulled Orin from the Poison Pond and turned him over, finding a look of horror on his face. He shoved the corpse into the waters, where it drifted for ten feet. Then several pairs of hands appeared from beneath the surface and pulled the body under, startling the onlookers.

"We should've decapitated him first," observed Noren, eyes scrutinizing Jenar. He seemed satisfied.

Unnerved and outraged by the suggestion, the knight spat silver into the grass. "What in Coiryn's name for? To desecrate the dead?"

Unmoved by the criticism, Noren replied, "To keep him dead, unless you're keen on meeting him again, maybe with supernatural powers that you will not be able to overcome."

Talon frowned. "Enough with speculation. We have what we came for. Back to Llurien, now."

The sorelia shook his head and turned from examining the knight's face and eyes. "If the Ever Fiend is truly dead, we must know. And it appears that killing him has killed all those under his control. This is revolutionary news, for the Ever Pathway may be safer than ever before. And you, Talon Stormbringer, will be famous across Llurien for having destroyed the dreaded Ever Fiend."

The Nyborian snorted. "I care nothing for fame, just my life. Mikolyn still needs help."

"I'm not sure that's true," the kryll admitted. The others turned to see that the ghastly wound in his side had turned silver, all signs of the blackened skin and frost gone.

"That looks worse, not better," Talon remarked, alarmed.

"Perhaps, but it doesn't hurt as before, or at all. I feel good, in fact."

Jenar nodded slowly, seeming much calmer, almost casual as she sat crossed legged now. "So do I. How can that be?" she asked Noren.

"I do not know," he admitted, "but on our return to Llurien, you can be examined. What of you, knight?"

Dal hesitated. "I feel fine but somehow sick inside all the same."

"Well enough to continue?"

The knight only frowned and Noren took it for acquiescence. Taking his sack of weapons, he started skirting the pond's edge, Nightwish walking beside him. The others looked to Talon and he reluctantly nodded. They still needed the karelia and examining the Fiend wouldn't take long. As he watched Jenar retrieve her swords, he saw the wisdom in doing something distasteful—he unsheathed his kryllan sword and quickly dipped it into the Poison Pond before following, the silver liquid dripping off its downward pointing tip as he walked. The knight and kryll exchanged a look and did the same with their sword and staff, respectively. Now they were armed for battle, should it come.

Talon kept alert as they approached the field of apparently dead-again minions. The spirits were still out there, though going by the diminished glow of lorenia lines on Noren's face, they might've been long gone. Nightwish showed few signs of wariness as he stepped around bodies with the sorelia, a sharply flicking tail revealing his distaste. Talon saw that every corpse had the same wound—a scorched and blackened cavity where a heart was, or in some cases, where it should've been. Some bore the distinct mark of a knife blade despite the absence of an actual dagger.

By silent agreement, the group stopped five paces from the seemingly dead Ever Fiend. Talon glanced at Noren, noticing no change to the lorenia lines. The sorelia met his gaze and nodded, so the Nyborian did what none of the others had the nerve to, though three of them had drunk from the sinister waters. That none of them wanted to go near the stuff again wasn't lost on him.

He approached the shrouded figure with sword at the ready, but it didn't move. To turn it over, he wasn't sure what to grab, for no limbs were apparent anymore, and he wondered if the cloak was enchanted in some way, but Noren likely would've told him if it was. As he hesitated, Nightwish brushed past him, grabbed the robe in his mouth, and pulled the Ever Fiend out to the pond's edge. Talon scratched the beast's black and green head a moment before leaning down to flip the carcass over. A sudden growl from the cat was his only warning as two pairs of silver coated hands burst from under the shimmering surface and roughly grabbed the Ever Fiend by the shoulders. With a violent jerk, the arms hauled the remains under the waters.

"It's time to leave this cursed place," Talon said, gray eyes stern.

"Yes," said Jenar, her voice sounding hollow to Talon's ears. She turned and began stepping over the bodies, leading them confidently. "This way."

Noren arched an eyebrow at her decisiveness as they followed. Talon kept scanning the bodies for some signs of movement but didn't see any. Even after they disappeared over a hill, he repeatedly glanced back, having taken rear guard with the knight. They walked in silence for some time, passing fallen bodies here and there as if everyone who had been tied to the Ever Fiend in some way had perished along with it. All bore a wound similar to those found collapsed by the pond.

Noren remarked that he was eager to return to the Poison Pond in the coming days because all those corpses would soon turn silver in decay. Soil enriched with this matter was called Ever Earth back on Llurien. Wizards used it for spells, but even common folk could plant something in it and achieve an unusual yield, not only in volume, but often in properties as well. It depended on what one planted in the stuff. The Nyborian thought this place was a source of too much that was evil in the world, more so than his childhood fairy tales had led him to believe.

"I feel unwell," the knight murmured to Talon, who eyed him. "I cannot place it. My mind is filled with regret."

Talon wasn't given much to introspection at his age. "I'd suggest a strong drink, but you've probably just consumed the strongest thing there is."

"No sooner had I drank it than this feeling came over me. I am ashamed."

Not understanding, Talon replied, "There's no shame in failing to resist the Ever Fiend's will."

"But you did. That is not what I mean. I am ashamed of my rank, and how I earned it." He sneered.

Talon's eyebrows rose. "You're a Knight of Coiryn!"

"I should not be," Dal admitted. "I have kept the secret for months but now I cannot bear it any longer. Stormbringer, you seem a man of honor and strength."

"As do you," he interrupted, only to hear Dal snort.

"Bards have even sung of my false deed. The hollowness of it all has grown on me."

Talon sensed that the knight was determined to unburden himself. He invoked the goddess of empathy. "I'm no

Priest of Darra to absolve you so you can enter Leisiran in death, if that is your worry."

"I know. Just hear my confession. You wished to know why I come to this place. I struck a bargain with the wizard. He cast an illusion that allowed me to seem brave as I fought and then chased off jhaikan, who seemingly fled through a Moon Gate to vanish. This happened before the Queen of Talendor so that I appeared to have saved her. For this I was promoted from Knight of the Valend to that of the Sword, and given the honorary Knight of Coiryn title."

Talon observed, "And these journeys into the Ever Pathways are the price you pay."

"You do not ask why I did it?"

"You don't strike me as a complicated man. It is self-evident."

The knight snorted bitterly. "I suppose so. And what am I now? A damned man lost on the Ever Pathways where he likely belongs."

"We are not lost or damned."

"I am. My shame grows with every accolade, and my honor is gone."

Talon did not disagree. "Some men have never had it."

The knight's face darkened. "Is it worse to have lost it?"

The Nyborian hadn't given it much thought but replied, "Lost honor can be regained by those who desire it. Those who never had it care nothing for acquiring it."

The knight gave him a long look. "Thank you, Talon Stormbringer. You have given me purpose. I will not die dishonored, if given the chance to redeem myself."

Talon noted that Dal's irises were turning silver and suspected that the knight's opportunities would be few. He seemed a decent man and Talon felt that he deserved a clean death, not whatever now awaited him. If it came to it, Talon would drive a sword straight through his heart rather than let him become one of the wretched denizens of this place. But even that might not put an end to him. Decapitation. That's what Noren had recommended. So be it.

The group ran across more bodies, this time a herd of harts. The woodland animals must've bounded through an open Ever Gate on their long legs by accident, for Talon couldn't imagine a scenario where such easily frightened game would pass through one on purpose. Surely no one brought them here as food, for this land corrupted anything that remained in it for too long; there was no telling what effect eating them would have. Every hart had an unexplained wound in its chest.

"It seems clear," began Mikolyn, "that by killing the Ever Fiend we have killed everything under his control."

Noren nodded. "The feel of this place is different now."

"How so?" Talon asked, though he sensed it himself.

"An oppressive weight has been lifted. Perhaps we have an opportunity."

Talon fixed a hard glare on him. "For what?"

"To reach the Black Tower and acquire its contents before anyone else does."

"The Ever Fiend's lair?" Mikolyn asked, looking intrigued. "It is said no one comes out alive."

"That's because of who lived there," replied the sorelia.

"You don't know that's the reason," Talon observed. "Anything could be guarding it."

"True, but it's plausible that with the Fiend and his minions dead, the way should be safer than at any other time. He could have set magical traps or something else still in effect, but the risk is worth taking."

The Nyborian asked, "Haven't you seen enough horror for today?"

Noren smiled. "I'm sorelian, the source of horror, according to some."

"What's inside this Black Tower?" the knight asked skeptically.

"No one knows," admitted Noren, "but if you were the Ever Fiend, ruling a vast land that's capable of turning any magic item into something more powerful, and even able to turn ordinary items into something special, would you not create and stockpile a vast supply of them?"

Jenar's eyes lit up. "I agree the risk is worth it. Come, Talon, we can have the most powerful weapons and armor known to exist."

He removed the hand she had laid on his arm, noting that it felt oddly cool to the touch and his skin remained cold where she had touched him. "Being forced to drink that terrible elixir taught you nothing?"

She shrugged. "I have cheated death."

"You do not know that. Something worse than death could be brewing inside you even now."

Jenar laughed vibrantly. "I feel fantastic. And if death, or worse, is already coming for me, then I must see this place first. Won't you come?"

"Entering a seemingly safe wizard's tower landed me in this mess. I'd rather not repeat the mistake."

"Stormbringer has a point," Dal admitted. "I say we return to Llurien."

Talon turned to the kryll. "Mikolyn?"

Sighing, Mikolyn's eyed Talon's sash full of silver elixir vials. "I do not have what I came for, the elixir. In all the chaos at the pond, I had forgotten. Regardless, this opportunity is unprecedented. It is worth investigating."

Noren smiled triumphantly. "Then it's settled. Even you, Stormbringer, cannot argue against majority rule. I have a general idea where the Black Tower is. We will have to search for it."

"No need. I know where it is," said Jenar. Seeing surprised expressions, she added apologetically, "Don't ask me how I know. I don't know myself."

The sorelia pursed his lips. "It appears that drinking the silver elixir has given you some ability to navigate the Ever Pathways."

Scowling, Talon observed, "Which means she can lead us out and we don't need you. Come, Jenar. Back to Llurien."

"Talon," she said, putting a caressing hand on his chest this time, gazing up at him through long lashes, "do this for me. Your strength can keep us safe, if that is truly what you desire."

"My strength would not be needed if we left this place."

She took his hand, squeezing it affectionately while she led them toward the Ever Fiend's Black Tower. Only the knight showed his reservations. No one had commented on his increasingly silver eyes. They seemingly knew the elixir's effect on Jenar. Mikolyn showed no ill effects, but his wound glowed faintly as if light shone from within. To Talon, all three of them had been poisoned. Orin might have been the luckiest of them, dead as he was. The Nyborian glanced back, but no one seemed to be behind them.

As they walked through field and forest, over hill and along another black river, Jenar commented on what lay before them and that each should be avoided for one reason or another. One forest had the dreaded kona leech plant, known for capturing people and keeping them alive while slowly drinking their blood for decades, except that here they fed on a victim's soul. On the horizon at another point stood the Jhaikan Grave, a vast, haunted battlefield where thousands of the vicious species had been slaughtered, though accounts differed on just who, or what, had done the killing. And finally they saw a small town with guard towers, a wall, and something humanoid milling about the lone entrance.

"That's one of the places we should avoid," Jenar remarked.

"I thought everyone is dead?" the knight asked, squinting. "Maybe there's something of use there."

She advised, "That's not a place for the Fiend's creatures. Those people you see over there are not under his control, which is why they're still alive. We are not alone."

"Then we should avoid them," Talon agreed.

"Indeed," said Noren, adding, "it's unlikely that anyone but us few realize what's happened and make for the Black Tower."

"It shouldn't be much longer," Jenar said, striding eagerly.

"That you know all of these things is troubling," Talon remarked. "How can we trust that you truly know the way?"

"Stormbringer has a point," remarked Dal, worry creasing his brow.

"Perhaps," began Mikolyn, "but she has identified places we've passed. Accurately, it seems."

"Indeed," Noren said. "I see no reason to doubt her."

"You're hardly without bias," Talon observed. "I doubt you'd care where we end up next as long as we stay in Everland. You seem to have no desire to return to Llurien."

"Nonsense," the sorelia replied. "I want the Black Tower's contents more than any bauble, as you'd once described items I can find on the Pathways. If I thought Jenar could not do it, I would not follow."

"But what makes you so sure she's leading us correctly?"

The karelia shrugged. "Nothing. But I have no reason to believe she is not. Do you?"

When the Nyborian only frowned, Jenar grinned, not taking offense at his questioning. "Have faith, Talon. I'm indebted to you and wouldn't risk your safety for nothing. You saved us all today."

"I wouldn't be so sure of that. Three of you drank and are already showing signs of something happening to you. And Orin is dead."

"Yes," agreed Mikolyn. "I've been wondering why he simply perished and we did not."

Noren shrugged. "His cowardice likely killed him."

Dal flushed and replied defensively, as if the remark had been about him, "I doubt that was the reason."

The sorelia gave him a knowing look and grinned hugely, and Talon wondered. Did Noren know of Dal's deal with the wizard? It seemed likely. He was Viland's partner in some way that Talon didn't understand. There was no telling what information he was privy to, but since the wizard and sorelia could choose who they sent into this place, it made sense that they chose together, using shared knowledge of the people they selected and whether they could be counted on or not. Or compelled to act one way or another. Noren probably knew things about each that the others wished he didn't.

The behavior of his companions had earned some of Talon's trust, but given that three of them had been tainted, and the sorelia had been born that way, Talon now trusted none of them. Relying on only himself was probably best, but then there was the troubling reality that either Noren or Jenar had to lead him from this place. Now that the sorelia had what he had come for originally, he had no need of Talon. Maybe Jenar's good graces were something Talon needed and he shouldn't show too much concern for her loyalties, at the risk of offending her.

Taking her bicep in one hand, and noticing how cold it was, he remarked casually, "I'm only concerned that you haven't had much chance to test the reliability of your new sense. You seem confident, which is good, but maybe you're being influenced by things we don't understand yet."

"You still have faith in me?" she asked playfully, leaning against him.

He smiled reassuringly and let the matter drop. "Of course."

They resumed walking, a rolling evergreen forest standing to one side for a time. The trees soon ended in a grassland, where a tower of gray limestone soared into the stormy air. It seemed out of place, no trails nearby and no reason for it to be here, but then everything here was peculiar. A low stone wall surrounded it, a broken wooden gate swinging freely on the side closest to them. They stopped and looked to Jenar, who indicated they had to pass by it to continue on their way. By silent agreement, they intended to steer clear.

As they approached, Talon saw the sorelia eyeing it curiously. "What is it?" he asked, hand on his sword hilt.

Noren began, "I think this is the—"

A woman's scream made them stop. All eyes turned to the tower's windows, from where it had come. After a glance at Talon that suggested this was a chance to redeem himself, the knight rushed forward while drawing his sword, shouting at them to help him save the woman, but no one else followed until the Nyborian took a step, too.

"No!" the sorelia urged him, grabbing his arm.

Scowling, Talon jerked free. "He can't go in there alone."

"No one should go in there."

"Too late," said Mikolyn ruefully, also advancing, his jhaikan-staff beginning to twirl casually as if he was warming up. Another scream split the air, sounding more terrified. Nightwish growled low in his throat.

Noren yelled at the knight, "Do not pass beyond the wall!" But Dal ignored the warning and charged by the broken gate onto the charred grass surrounding the tower.

"I think he might be right," said Jenar to Talon, following him. "It's better to steer clear, unless one of you can operate a Moon Gate."

That stopped the Nyborian. "A Moon Gate? What do you mean?"

Nodding at the building before them, she remarked, "It's the only way to enter the Vanishing Tower without waiting for it to appear before you. There's one inside so that we can use another to arrive there if we had it. But if we enter, we could use it to reach the Black Tower's Moon Gate in seconds."

Talon arched an eyebrow at the sorelia, who nodded.

"Yes, I can control one, of course. We'd have to hurry before the tower disappears." He began running for it, the sack of weapons he had been carrying making a racket. Jenar smirked and ran, too, with a scowling Talon bringing up the rear, the great cat loping beside him.

"Why would the tower disappear?" he yelled, seeing the knight bash open the door and fearlessly enter.

But no sooner had he said it than the whole building, grass, and wall surrounding it began to shimmer. The kryll nearly stepped over the perimeter but stopped himself. Moments later, the place had vanished, with the knight inside.

CHAPTER SIX

THE BLACK TOWER

Talon's knuckles were white on the sword hilt in its scabbard, his grim glare keeping the others from talking to him. Noren had explained that the infamous Vanishing Tower was unlikely to appear in the same place any time soon and that the knight was probably lost forever. He might escape the building, but if he did, he could be anywhere in Everland. They'd never see him again, it seemed, assuming he even survived. That glow in Dal's eyes had Talon certain that the knight would never leave this place regardless. Still, he had wanted to help the doomed man, and even Jenar's assurances that it was really Dal's own fault for charging in there did nothing to cheer him. He wanted out of this place.

Instead, they were headed for the Black Tower. If Talon could reach the Moon Gate there, he might still rescue the knight. He strode with greater purpose, nearly leaving the others behind.

Along the way, they passed an Ever Gate—one of several they'd seen, light or dark depending on whether it was day or night on the other side. They steered clear, both Noren and Jenar saying it wasn't the one which led back to the wizard who'd sent them here. Talon approached anyway and gazed out, seeing a seemingly impassable jungle lit by the sun, suggesting they must've been on the far side of the world.

Within an hour, they crested a hill to see the Black Tower in the distance, obsidian walls glistening as if wet and oozing. Before it stood the Black Grove, which stretched toward them and from right to left a great distance, the trees still as death, not a leaf rippling. Beyond it all rose a wall of mist that Noren said came from the Misty Cliff on the far side. No one knew what lay at its bottom, and the fog obscured whatever stood beyond it, if anything. Talon remembered it from the vision Viland had given him. Aside from lights twinkling in just one of the tower's windows, there were no signs of life.

Or death.

"Should we be worried that nothing appears to guard it?" Talon asked.

Jenar said, "No. The trees do that." At his dubious look, she smiled. "You'll see."

He reached for his sword but she stayed his hand and led them onward. A glance at Nightwish showed the cat's ears mostly forward but sometimes swiveling back or to the sides. The cat was on high alert and Talon had long ago learned to trust the instincts of animals. This one was made of stern stuff, for rumor had it that even battle-trained horses could not lightly be made to enter the pathways.

They followed a path that led straight toward the grove, where Talon detected the faint smell of blood. Nightwish growled and the Nyborian pulled out his sword, noticing the lorenia lines on Noren's face glowing softly. With the tall evergreens looming over them, all but Jenar stopped. The trees had black trunks and dark red leaves, which Noren eyed greedily. The karelia approached a tree as if to pull a leaf, but Jenar spoke like she had eyes in the back of her head.

"Don't."

The sorelia paused. "Explain."

"Take a leaf from the ground if you want, but unless you want to provoke the Linganore trees, I wouldn't pluck one."

Noren watched her step on the path through the forest and sighed, following with the others. The turbulent sky disappeared behind the thick canopy as they entered the Black Grove, but they'd only gone twenty paces when the path abruptly ended. Jenar walked forward anyway, and as she neared the boles, they rose on their roots and shuffled aside, letting her through. She calmly suggested that her companions hurry and they closed the gap with her, none of them failing to notice the trees gathering behind them as if to cut off escape. The trees continued to part ahead and close behind so that the travelers walked in a perpetual circle of foliage. No one spoke, their wary eyes saying all that was needed.

And those eyes widened when the trees parted once more to reveal a sickening sight. A thick, black branch hung over the path. A pulsating kona leech plant had entwined itself there, and in its grip lay a wide-eyed and staring man, his horrified eyes imploring them for help as the plant crushed him against the branch lengthwise. He appeared to be hugging it from beneath. One arm dangled toward the ground, the hand twitching toward them. The plant's green leaves shone with luster, a pod-like nest enveloping its victim as tentacled vines gripped the Linganore tree. A few unoccupied vines sensed the newcomers. They unwound and poised like snakes, one lashing out toward them.

Talon had seen this before during an excursion into Valley Wood. He severed a vine, which fell past him, oozing black ichor instead of the expected blood the plant usually drained from its prey. Not waiting for further attacks, he leapt forward with steel flashing and severed first one vine, then another. Striving to save itself, the plant tried to disgorge its victim, but it was too slow, allowing Talon to shear off a hunk perilously close to the man. The plant seemed to shriek as if alive. Unnerved, Talon waited a precious second for the victim to fall helplessly to the ground, giving him a free swing at the kona leech. With a clean stroke, careful not to strike the tree in case it, too, should join in attacking him, Talon cut the bloodsucking plant in half. As it landed, he made short work of the dying plant until a dozen pieces lay scattered around.

Mikolyn went to the fallen man to help him up, but the plant's victim shrank back, staring in horror toward the group.

"Ever...Ever...F-f-f-Fiend!" he stammered.

The Nyborian looked back in alarm but saw no one but his companions. "The Fiend is dead." He faced the man again but saw sightless eyes gazing into oblivion.

"And so is he," remarked Noren. "We were too late. That plant was feeding on his soul, not his blood as they do on Llurien. I wonder how long he's been here."

"Long enough to go insane," remarked Jenar quietly.

"What should we do?" Mikolyn asked.

"Behead him," answered Noren. "And not dawdle."

Talon grimaced at the butchery he was about to do, but with a clean stroke he severed the head from the body. He wiped his blade on the man's shirt and rose. Then he approached the trees, expecting them to part, but they did not. Then Jenar approached the boles, which shuffled aside while she flashed a grin at him.

Nothing more happened within the grove. They escaped to the far side where the wide Black Tower soared a thousand feet into the stormy sky. An additional twenty-eight small towers rose a hundred feet up from the main tower's side, each topped with a colored minaret. Their number matched that of the gods. That couldn't be a coincidence.

"There appears to be no way in," remarked the kryll.

Jenar nodded. "Not to most, but I know the way. There's no ground floor entrance unless you know what to do."

Talon followed with his sword drawn as they strode up to the Ever Fiend's home. He wondered what had happened to the companions of the kona leech plant's victim. They hadn't seen another such plant. Like some denizens of this place, did it, too, get here by accident? A grove of such creatures might be advantageous to the Ever Fiend, but then no one knew what the Fiend wanted, despite all the stories about it appearing on Llurien to steal this or that—often a living person, or so the bedtime stories said. Maybe the kryllan species knew, for they had an expert on almost everything in their ranks.

Jenar stopped before the Black Tower and appeared to carefully choose a blank spot, where she traced a vertical rectangle with a small circle at each corner. Then she drew a line from one corner of the rectangle to the opposite corner, and another line connecting the remaining two corners. Inside the rectangle she drew a triangle, and where its three points touched the rectangle, she again drew a small circle. In the center of the rectangle, she drew a large circle. Once this part was complete, the pattern glowed silver, the invisible door on which she had drawn this diagram sliding upward to reveal only blackness beyond.

Talon recognized the symbol as one associated with the gods. Was the Black Tower a doorway to their realm? The key to this place? A meeting spot? Or a place where horrible people were banished instead of tortured forever in Lochiare, damned to eternal boredom in Maeryndor, or their soul ripped apart in E'Kainum? Some had wondered if

Everland was yet another afterlife for the evil, but the gods would confirm nothing.

"I'm surprised it's that easy to enter such a formidable place," said Noren.

Jenar smiled wanly. "It only works because I drank from the Poison Pond and have the elixir in my system. That, and I have some magic talent."

"Interesting, albeit a steep price to pay."

"Hopefully there's no other price," remarked Talon, concerned for Jenar. Her skin seemed darker than before, but then that could've just been the lighting conditions. He spoke the word of magic which triggered the Ball of Light valender and a fist-sized orb appeared, bobbing in the air a few feet above and in front of his head. He had no doubt about it now—Jenar's skin had darkened as if she had gotten tanned by the sun in the last hour. He moved toward the opening as the light kept ahead of him, the others following.

As light filled the interior, Talon scanned for indications of danger that didn't appear. The smell of decay seemed to permeate the dank air, the source undetected. No sound came from anywhere. To the left and right stood hallways and before them descended a wide staircase. Another rose beside it into blackness.

"Where are these items we're risking our lives for?" he asked with disdain. He had made a living as a thief of late, but there was a limit to how much risk he took for that, and they'd far exceeded it.

"This way." Jenar brushed by him.

Talon had expected them to go up, but instead they descended deeper and deeper, through empty corridors and abandoned rooms. Nothing seemed to have been there in forever, thick cobwebs in corners and undisturbed dust everywhere. One large room bore a huge table with the symbol Jenar had traced earlier carved into its surface.

Twenty-eight chairs surrounded it. The furniture looked as if it had not been used in eons and had been styled in ways he found bizarre and unsettling, though he couldn't pinpoint why.

They reached a set of closed but unlocked double doors, both carved with a scene of wizards and warriors who bore features unlike any they'd seen. But then perhaps they were from other continents on Llurien. Jenar grinned at him before shoving open the doors. Beyond lay a room large enough to obscure the far side. Close to them, down a short flight of steps, were piles of weapons, organized by type. Swords, knives, and daggers lay in one, axes in another, hammers, flails, and maces farther away, spears and lances elsewhere, and great piles of arrows, crossbows, and both long and short bows. Along the walls stood suits of armor, and above the armor, more weapons occupied all the available wall space.

With a word, Noren took command of Talon's ball of light and split it into a dozen orbs that flew outward to positions near and far in the hall, illuminating its entirety. A murmur of appreciation escaped Mikolyn's lips, for the piles nearest them were duplicated several times across the vast sweep of the room, in the center of which stood a large dais as if a speaker would address a crowd from there. A Moon Gate stood at its center, the lack of a shimmering vista through its frame indicating it was off. Talon sighed in relief at its presence, wanting to head straight for it and find Dal.

The group descended to the weapon-strewn floor. Talon continued to the gate, though Noren was the only one who could cast the spell to activate it. With the tower deserted, they could have the time to get Dal and return, and then be done with this place.

Jenar joined him, as did Noren, each looking around and enjoying the vantage point. Nightwish roamed among the piles, pawing at odd items, while Mikolyn went to a pile of jhaikan-staffs, which he began looking through.

"I guess there's no way to tell," he began, "what any of these items do."

"Not until you use it, no," agreed the sorelia, who dropped the sack he had been carrying, eyes on the treasures before them.

The kryll asked, "Any chance that this Moon Gate is the kind that can be made to go to any other Moon Gate? Imagine taking all of this to Llurien."

Noren put his hands on the metal gate's rectangular frame and began examining it. Talon hoped the answer was no. The last thing Llurien needed was such a treasure trove of cursed items being let loose, and the sorelia had already admitted that was exactly what he wanted. Noren indicated the gate only went to one place, as far as he knew, so Talon suggested activating it so they could go find the knight. The sorelia frowned, Jenar seemed indifferent, but the kryll nodded his agreement, so Noren cast the spell and the gate shimmered to life, a glistening wall of silver offering an occasional glimpse of the destination—another room devoid of significance to them.

They gathered on the dais, calling Nightwish over, and were about to step through when the room lights dimmed. The mynx growled and backed away from the room's entrance, where a black robed and cowled figure drifted down the stairs. It looked just like the limbless Ever Fiend that Talon had killed at the Poison Pond, though it seemed somehow bigger, more intimidating. Only darkness filled the hood, but Talon could sense when their eyes met, a jolt of menace striking him.

"We killed you!" said Mikolyn, reaching for his jhaikan-staff. One hand went to the wound in his side, where the silver light began to grow brighter while he gasped in pain.

The figure glided to a stop not far from the dais, sur-rounded by weapons, the deadliest of which was itself. "No," it said, hollow voice echoing whereas theirs did not, "you killed Aeonyn, an apprentice."

A murmur escaped the sorelia. "More than one Ever Fiend? By the gods. We must tell Llurien."

Talon agreed but doubted they'd get the chance unless they went through the Moon Gate and somehow destroyed it so they couldn't be followed. Stalling, he asked the Fiend, "How many of you?"

"You will learn soon enough when you join them. All but you." The Ever Fiend raised a ghostly hand at the kryll. Mikolyn lifted from the floor with the motion, a burst of light erupting from his wound as he screamed in agony. Then the Fiend jerked its wrist and Mikolyn flew off the dais and into a suit of plate armor on a stand, which fell atop him, pinning him to the floor. When he lost con-sciousness, the wound's light began to fade and Talon feared he was dead.

"Why not the kryll?" Talon asked, one hand discreetly drawing the Chaos Blade at his waist.

"He had no magic talent," came the answer. "I can sense magic in all of you. One drink from the—"

Talon didn't wait for him to finish, hurling the en-chanted blade. The Ever Fiend let the blade slam into its heart. It remained standing, calmly, and didn't even glance down while the weapon slowly exited the wound as if pulled out by an invisible hand. It clattered to the floor, steaming black ichor covering its length. Thinking like Noren for a moment, Talon briefly wondered what the stuff would be worth to a wizard, but as he watched, it boiled off the dagger and dissipated. From the hole in the Ever Fiend's chest, silver light gleamed until the wound closed as if it had never been there, even the robe mending itself.

Behind him, the Nyborian noticed Nightwish dragging Mikolyn from under the armor. The cat had little trouble, strong as he was, and the kryll began to stir. Jenar hadn't even drawn a sword; her lips were moving silently as if praying to some god. Beside the Moon Gate, Noren began to quietly speak strange words in karelian, the lorenia lines on his face glowing brighter.

Hoping to distract the Ever Fiend from Noren's actions, Talon descended the dais to a pile of spears and took one. "Something in here must kill you."

The Fiend laughed. "You are welcome to try, Stormbringer. Nothing in here has ever worked."

Talon arched an eyebrow. The Fiend sounded disappointed. Perhaps he could lend assistance. "Maybe the right person hasn't attacked you."

The Ever Fiend gestured at the piles. "Every weapon is different. Perhaps I'll let you try them all."

Talon hurled the weapon with all his might. The Fiend never moved as the spear struck it full in the face, the momentum throwing it backward to the floor.

CHAPTER SEVEN

AN OLD TALENT

Jenar gasped, and when Talon looked at her, she seemed aghast. Had *she* wanted to strike the Ever Fiend down? He ascended the dais again to speak to her when movement brought his gaze back to the Ever Fiend. The spear pushed up by itself and fell to one side. Then the Fiend silently rose to its previous position, seemingly unharmed. Talon felt that the only smart move was to rush through the Moon Gate and run for their lives. But Noren had another idea.

"You must go while I delay the Fiend," said the sorelia to him, the lorenia lines on his face and neck glowing so intensely that Talon almost couldn't see his eyes. "Take Nightwish. The world must learn there's more than one Fiend."

"You can tell just as well as I," responded Talon, surprised the karelia was willing to sacrifice himself, especially to such a fate. Who knew for how many eons Noren would be the Ever Fiend's slave?

Noren smiled without humor. "Who would believe a sorelia? Take my sword. You will need it more than I."

"The Fiend will destroy your soul." Talon reluctantly took the offered blade.

"You forget I'm karelian. I have already separated it from my body, which will battle the Fiend, and when it falls, my soul shall escape."

Talon remembered the words of magic the karelia had spoken. Karelia could willfully separate their souls from their bodies and still control both, a feat usually done when death is certain and there's some chance the soul won't reach an afterlife if it's still in the body at death. As gods-appointed caretakers of all spiritual matters on Llurien, the karelia tracked down ghosts and sent them to the afterlife. They blasted undead back to the grave. They communicated with the dead when necessary. Noren had done the dreaded spell—his spirit hovered nearby, ready to flee from the Ever Fiend's grasp the moment his body died.

Talon hesitated to leave him behind, but as Mikolyn staggered to the top of the dais beside the still open Moon Gate, Noren gave a sharply spoken command to Nightwish and the big cat reared up, pushing the kryll through the gate's opening with both paws before leaping into Talon and Jenar, propelling all three of them through and leaving Noren behind. Just before they vanished from one tower to arrive in the other, words of magic from both sorelia and Ever Fiend filled the air, accompanied by a whoosh, a boom of thunder, and a scream. The sound cut off as they left the treasure room into what looked like a throne room. Three gilded chairs stood at one end, faded banners and tapestries hanging from the gray limestone walls. Talon stopped himself from stumbling to the floor, one hand in Nightwish's dark fur and the other around Jenar's arm. Behind them, the Moon Gate remained on.

"We must go back," said Jenar, turning toward it. Talon shoved her forward and away.

"No. We must honor Noren's sacrifice. Hurry, away from this gate and out of this tower."

"But we are far from Talendor," Mikolyn protested weakly, rising to his feet with a grimace.

Talon helped him up. "It doesn't matter. The first chance to escape to Llurien, we take it, wrong Ever Gate or not."

With the cat and the kryll following, he forced a still protesting Jenar from the room. The Moon Gate continued shimmering as they escaped into a hall with a stairway curling down the tower. The Nyborian peered through a window on their way and saw the familiar stone wall around the Vanishing Tower, confirming their location. That meant Dal was around here somewhere, if he still lived, and Talon felt eager to find and save the knight.

As they descended from the building's pinnacle, Jenar's resistance faded and she began to lead the way, remarking that there was a way to know their whereabouts. On reaching the second floor, having passed all other rooms and doorways without stopping, she pushed into a central, circular room where a glowing orb four feet in diameter had been set into a circular, waist-high table of obsidian, where it floated. An image of blue covered much of the orb's surface, but a number of large, irregular shapes of brown and green did, too, and only on nearing it did Talon recognize one as the continent Antaria, from whence they'd come.

"A map," he said, watching in fascination as the orb suddenly swirled several seconds before stopping.

"The tower just changed locations," observed Jenar. "That's what the Orb of Vessyn does."

"It shows where on Llurien we are near?"

"It's actually what's causing the tower to change locations. It's supposed to stay in one place unless someone makes it move, but this place corrupts everything magical, so it does whatever it wants now. It has for centuries."

"Fascinating," Mikolyn said, sounding weak and clutching his side. "I've heard of the orb. It's legendary. No one's known what happened to it."

Talon didn't share his amazement. He gazed at it and didn't recognize the continent they were on now, but Jenar touched the shining surface and the word "Llorus" appeared in white letters. She pressed a small mountain range and the words "Tissan Peaks" shown atop them. She placed both hands on it, causing the view to get much closer so that a walled town appeared, the word "Nieve" above it when she touched it. Letting her hand linger, the orb emitted a short burst of light.

"We just moved to there, in the Kingdom of Baeshor," Jenar remarked.

"We can control it?" Talon asked, excited by the chance to go where they needed so quickly.

"Seems like it."

"Good. Back to Talendor!"

So engrossed in the display was Talon that he didn't hear a metal-shod foot strike the stone floor behind them until nearly too late, a growl from Nightwish confirming that an enemy approached. Two more steps sounded, nearing him, as he turned and began to raise Noren's sword to ward off the gleaming long sword that slashed down at him. Mikolyn was faster, or had heard the knight sooner, for the jhaikan-staff flashed upward to block the blade and turn it aside.

"Dal!" Talon yelled, relieved but confused by the attack—until he saw the silver light shining from the man's eyes and a look of wrath twisting his features. The knight wasted no time, sword swinging again, but this time for Mikolyn, who'd seemingly spent his last bit of strength in saving the Nyborian. The blade sheared through the kryll's shoulder and halfway through his torso, killing him. Dal tried to pull the blade free but it was stuck in bone and sinew. Talon hesitated, remembering his vow to decapitate the now undead knight rather than leave him to this fate.

Jenar leapt forward, twin swords ripping through Dal's armor like it was no more than cloth. Both weapons now revealed the awful power granted by the Poison Pond: one left a trail of sizzling silver liquid in its wake, flesh charring at the touch, while the other caused everything within six inches of the wound it left to freeze solid. Nightwish bore the knight to the stone floor only to have the frozen half of Dal's torso shatter on impact, the eerie light quickly fading from his staring eyes.

For a moment no one moved, as Talon stood wondering what had happened to the knight and the woman he had come to rescue. Then a voice spoke near the door.

"Stormbringer, you must escape the tower now!"

Talon's eyes scanned for the source, which began to coalesce before him as Nightwish rose to all fours alertly but not indicating danger. The familiar sight of Noren materialized, but only as a ghostly phantasm, a soft white glow surrounding him.

"You are dead?" Talon asked in concern.

"No, but I am defeated and held in thrall so he can take me to the Poison Pond. He comes here now for you. Flee before he reaches this room and sees where you —"

Suddenly Noren let out a shriek, his face and body contorting in pain, eyes bulging in horror. The screaming continued as his spirit flew backwards from the room as if hauled away by an invisible force. They could hear the sound of his fast passage up and away to the tower's top before the anguished cries abruptly cut off.

Talon turned back to the orb and Jenar said, "We're on Namaera now, on the other side of the world."

"Not for long." He moved the orb until it showed the southern edge of Antaria, then zoomed in near Talendor, but he didn't have Jenar's expertise with the device and accidentally made the tower stop near, but not near enough, to their target. The orb gave a flash.

Jenar glanced upward. "He's here. I can sense him."

Talon grabbed her arm and fled with Nightwish from the room, down a flight of stairs, and out into the grass surrounding the Vanishing Tower. He had never thought to be happy to see the landscape of Everland. They ran through the broken wooden gate and escaped into an open field, sprinting for some distance before stopping. When they looked behind, the tower was gone again. There was no sign of the Ever Fiend.

"Which way?" Talon asked.

Jenar pointed and the three survivors began a fast walk, having a few hours to go, and only now did Talon begin to realize his fatigue, having lost all sense of time and space. As before, the landscape sometimes changed without warning, making Talon swear he would never enter this place again. He hadn't realized how much comfort there lay in a mountain that stayed put, or a forest that didn't come alive, or even a river of thirst-quenching water instead of black ichor.

Nightwish suddenly went alert beside them and they moved behind a bush to peer over the crest of a hill. Before them were the Shadow Riders who'd left the bridge before their fight. Only six of them remained and they no longer moved in a tight formation. Instead they milled about, as if uncertain of what to do or where to go. Their leader, he with the Shadow Horn and lance with pennant, sat still atop his steed, eyes staring vacantly, but at times he seemed to perk up as if hearing something in the distance, his black horse moving restlessly beneath him.

"We must get by them," said Jenar, fingering her cursed swords.

"They seem lost."

She nodded. "Maybe the Ever Fiend we killed controlled them and they are without a master."

"For now. This might make it easier to destroy them."

She smiled at him, the first time she had shown humor in a while. "Let's find out."

CHAPTER EIGHT

THE CURSE OF POWER

Talon and Jenar spent a few moments planning an attack that relied on Nightwish. He made use of the riders being in a small valley, taller hills on each side of them. Their poor positioning would've surprised him were it not for their general disorientation.

Leaving Jenar where she was, he and Nightwish crouched low and skirted the riders' position until they were on the opposite side of them. With his years of sneaking around, the Nyborian was nearly as silent as the beast, his supple leather never creaking. Once in position, Talon sent the cat over the hill with a command to be at ease and only counterattack, for he hoped that no battle frenzy would start immediately. As expected, the horsemen turned toward Nightwish, their attention on the cat, and as he had hoped, they'd come alert but not charged the seemingly unthreatening animal. Talon moved back toward Jenar but stopped halfway so that they surrounded their prey on three sides, but neither human showed themselves.

That changed when Jenar quietly rose with twin swords in hand and began advancing on the riders from behind. Nightwish's presence provided the distraction

Jenar needed to approach them. Talon watched for the right moment, which came when one of the rear horses whinnied and began to turn as if having sensed the danger from behind. With a battle cry, Talon rose and ran over the hill's crest into view, plunging toward the nearest rider, who swiveled in his direction. Talon's rush carried him past Nightwish, to whom he shouted an attack command. The cat leapt two strides forward and bore that rider and horse to the ground with a growl and ripped apart the horse's throat with claws. Talon threw a dagger at the rider, who it struck in the eye, felling him.

Jenar slashed the back legs of the horse before her and it crumpled to the ground, one leg burned and the other frosted. Another swing and the rider's head rolled across the ground.

Talon grew alarmed on seeing the leader of the riders lifting the Shadow Horn to its lips. More riders converging on them would surely mean death. Without breaking stride, he desperately hurled Noren's black sword, which twirled end over end like all those daggers he had spent a decade practicing with. Only training and instinct gave him any hope that the longer weapon would fly as intended. It didn't, piercing the rider's leg instead of his heart, but that was enough. Green flames erupted from the sword and soon engulfed both screaming rider and frenzied horse. Both burst into a cloud of ash and fell to the ground, the magical horn and sword landing in the pile.

Only three riders were left, but two bolted for freedom. To Talon's surprise, Jenar shouted words he didn't recognize and both steeds stopped so violently that their riders flew over their heads to crash on the ground. He quickly grabbed up Noren's sword again and raced beside her to the fallen riders, who rose to meet their attack. They'd been Coiryn Riders before Everland and the Ever Fiend had corrupted them, and such horseman specialized in fighting on horseback. Afoot, neither was a match for the pair who now dispatched them in a dozen blows. Behind them, Nightwish had taken down the remaining horse and then clawed apart the last rider, several more dents on his battle armor.

Only two horses remained alive, if they could be called that. Neither had moved since Jenar's command and Talon got his first good look at them. Both were jet black, their coats shimmering with unnatural luster, almost beautiful despite their air of wild, evil vibrancy. On a hunch, he cut a strand from the mane of a dead horse and tucked it into his belt. Perhaps the mane of a Shadow Rider's horse had some value.

"Good for you." Jenar approved, grinning. "Maybe you're returning to your old, thieving self. Not everything here is so bad, is it?"

"Yes, it is. How did you stop the horses like that?"

She shrugged. "The words to command them came into my mind. How did you know to control Nightwish?" she challenged playfully, seeming amused by her new skills.

"My father was a knight and the cats are part of the military in Nybor. I learned their commands as a matter of course."

She patted a sable steed. "Let's ride these to the gate. They'll obey me. It'll be much faster."

Little surprised the Nyborian anymore and he retrieved the Shadow Horn before approaching a horse, which looked back at him with silvery eyes that left little doubt that it had drunk from the Poison Pond. He gave it the once-over as Jenar casually mounted hers, and then he did the same, half expecting the horse to bolt. It didn't. He barely had time to grab the reins and stow Noren's sword before Jenar shouted commands and they sped off, Nightwish loping along beside them.

As they charged over fields and through forests, nothing challenged the pair. Figures in the distance scattered on seeing them. Any vegetation that might've been alive and intent on molesting them did nothing. They leapt over black creeks, charged over hills, and cantered beneath that stormy sky that never unleashed anything but dread on the pair who trod under it. After a short time, they slowed on Jenar's command and soon saw an Ever Gate on the ground before them, its rectangular outline filled with light. While Talon had lost all track of time, it didn't surprise him that day had arrived on Llurien.

The pair dismounted before Jenar sent their hideous steeds galloping away. He decided not to ask the creatures' destination, for all that mattered now was a return to the normalcy of Llurien. One last glance around showed they were alone, and then the pair stepped into the opening, with Nightwish trailing along.

No sooner had they stepped from Everland into the shadows of Viland's courtyard than Talon felt relief wash over him. A blue sky had never seemed so welcome, the fresh ocean air off the coast of Talendor so invigorating. He took Jenar's hand and found her turning toward him, an excited light in her eyes. He crushed her lips in a deep kiss, pent-up longing for life and its more pleasurable pursuits overcoming him. But the coldness of that kiss startled him. He disengaged and was about to ask how she felt when a voice stopped him.

"Only the two of you?" asked Viland, sounding surprised, arms folded. "What of Noren?"

"Dead," answered Talon sadly, "or worse. The Ever Fiend has him."

The wizard's eyebrows shot up. "You met the Ever Fiend?" With a word of magic and swing of his fist, he made the Ever Gate behind them close, as if he were afraid something—or someone—might come through. Then he gestured for them to follow into the courtyard and back up into his tower and the living quarters therein. Along the way, Talon and Jenar related what had occurred, leaving out certain parts, like that Jenar had consumed the silver elixir. When Viland extended one greedy hand for the elixir vials, Talon hesitated.

"What do you do with this? I've seen it destroy men."

The wizard nodded. "Then you know that I was right in telling you not to touch it. Fear not, Nyborian. I merely use it in my spells. I certainly don't consume it or force others to do the same. As you say, it is death, or worse. A drop here or there in spells makes them stronger. Whether the spell is for good or evil makes no difference, so the elixir itself is not your cause for concern, but the character of the wizard."

Talon stared him in the eyes. "Now you know why I ask."

A chuckle escaped Viland. "I do enjoy a good repartee. I'd not expect such from you were it not for your upbring-ing. Years as a squire in the courts of Nybor has given you more sophistication than most would expect. It's a shame about your parents. You seem to have the makings of a fine knight. I inquired about you in your absence, you see. It is not too late for you, Stormbringer, given your honor." See-ing Talon frown, he added, "Hide it all you will. It lives inside you still."

"A poet," remarked Jenar with a snicker, one arm wrapped around Talon's waist. She jingled the sash holding the vials on his torso and looked at Viland suggestively. "Are you sure you don't want a sip? It's not all bad."

Neither man shared her amusement, the wizard ex-tending a black hand once more. He didn't seem to realize her admission to having consumed some. "Those are mine by right, Nyborian."

Talon sighed and handed them over. He hadn't expected the wizard's comments about honor, especially those seeming to praise him for it. Maybe the rumors about the man were unfounded. Nothing he had witnessed personally seemed nefarious, other than the basic mission, and by contrast to the beings inside Everland, Viland was downright cordial, though Talon was no stranger to two-faced people. Still, there was nothing to be done for it and he had to just hope nothing evil came of his delivery.

When the wizard suggested that he return to the Poison Pond later for more elixir, Talon glared so forcefully that the wizard took a step back and dropped the subject before smiling as if to apologize.

The Nyborian made no mention of the other items he had collected along the way, though Viland noticed the Shadow Horn only to have Talon sternly shake his head that it was not for the taking. He also saw the sorelian sword at Talon's hip, making an inquiry about acquiring it only to be rebuffed. Talon intended to find a way to honor Noren, who had sacrificed himself for their lives, in defiance of everything Talon had ever heard about the sorelia. He would never look at another quite the same. Perhaps some good remained in those corrupted members of the noble karelian species.

Night began to fall outside and Viland offered them a pair of rooms, but Jenar made it clear she intended to celebrate life with Talon. They retired to his spacious suite overlooking the courtyard and that silent corner below where a portal to a dread world lurked unseen. Nightwish, who now showed all signs of having allegiance to a grateful Talon, lay silently at the foot of the bed while Jenar stoked a large fire, admitting she felt cold and wanting Talon to warm her with his body.

She insisted on pulling curtains around the four-post bed as if to shield herself from the light, acting coy about her shyness when teased about it. Only then did she undress, and in the black shadows, her skin seemed only as dark as his. The first touch of her cold skin no longer surprised him and he vowed to warm her up the old fashioned way. She otherwise seemed more alive than any woman he had been with in his short years, almost as if possessed. The drink flowed easily before and after their passionate tryst. He fell into a deep sleep with her nude body, still chill to the touch, pressed against his flesh.

He awoke sometime later, a growl from Nightwish disturbing him even as he realized the cat had climbed onto the bed, the ponderous weight shifting the mattress, the bed frame creaking. His eyes opened to find the black and green mynx about to lick his face. He pushed the beast aside and sat up, a glance revealing that they were alone. Where had the woman gone? To stoke the fire, which had died down? A moment later, the cat's ears pointed toward the window overlooking the courtyard. Talon caught the faint sound of words, the inflection telling him that magic was afoot. He rose, naked, and grabbed Noren's sword instead of his from the bedside, and gazed down to the ground.

In the courtyard's corner, the Ever Gate blazed with shimmering light. Before it, Viland stood with arms falling to his sides, his spell complete. Beside him, a figure with black skin and wild long hair stood with a dagger at the wizard's back.

"Viland!" Talon called, wondering what else to do from here. He had no bow to take out the creature beside the man.

The wizard turned his dark face up, an expression of horror on it. Then the figure beside him looked up, too, and Talon gasped. Something had transformed Jenar into a being not unlike those they'd seen in Everland, but she bore more resemblance to one in particular than any other.

She smiled obscenely at him, silver light shining from her eyes while she pressed one hand to her belly.

"You're to be a father, Talon!" Jenar called, her voice deep and hollow. "I feel him growing already. No telling what powers this one will have!"

He cried out in shock, desperate to save Jenar but powerless to stop her from carrying out her actions. Had the silver elixir been turning her into this all along? Had she known? Was everything she had done since drinking it just a ruse to deliver them one by one to the Ever Fiend? He didn't want to believe it, that this vivacious woman he had just shared a bed with had been a predator, possibly since drinking from the Poison Pond. Compassion made his heart wrench. If only he had a long bow, he could've destroyed her now rather than let her become some minion of the Fiend in Everland, possibly forever.

And a baby. He was to be a father of some unholy creature? It couldn't be true. And yet somehow he sensed it was. How was he to walk this Llurien knowing some abomination he had wrought would wander those Ever Pathways, possibly coming to Llurien from time to time to do who knows what to the living? Something must be done.

Jenar turned toward the Ever Gate and jabbed the blade in Viland's back, urging him forward. Talon turned and dashed from the room in all his glory, leaping down the steps with Nightwish close behind. On reaching the courtyard, he felt no surprise that both Jenar and Viland were gone, but the Ever Gate remained open and he strode up to it and peered through. Not twenty yards beyond, Jenar delivered the wizard to the waiting Ever Fiend, who grasped a vial of shining liquid and forced it to Viland's lips as he arched the man backward, the silver elixir emptying down his throat. Viland fell to the ground, clutching at his neck and convulsing.

Jenar paid him no mind as the Fiend draped a hooded robe around her, and she bowed her head. Then she raised her chin and turned toward the Nyborian. A brief flash of silver eyes came from within the dark recesses of the hood. She beckoned and the Shadow Riders came at her call, black steeds moving in tight formation once more. Only then did Talon remember the Shadow Horn, his eyes darting to the bedroom above. Jenar made no indication that she had taken it as she mounted one horse.

Silently, Viland stopped writhing and rose to his feet before the Ever Fiend draped a cowled robe around him. He climbed atop another nightmare horse and Talon wondered if he was the only person to see three Ever Fiends at the same time. That he could've been one chilled him, for it seemed clear that anyone with magic talent became a Fiend if they had consumed the silver elixir. What had become of Noren?

The horses wheeled as one and rode away. The master Fiend turned toward the gate and Talon beyond. It began to glide forward. Talon raised the black sword in his hand, fearing it would not be enough for the Ever Fiend. The Ever Gate might be another matter.

He slashed at its edge and saw the blade ignite with green flames as it contacted the seemingly insubstantial portal. The Ever Fiend stopped as black flame sprang from the portal frame and the Nyborian took his cue, swinging with all his might at every edge that shimmered before him. Time after time the blade cut into the gate. Soon a wall of black flame engulfed it from all sides as man and mynx backed away from the searing heat. As the gate hissed, popped, and crackled into oblivion, the Ever Fiend's final words came through it and sent a chill down his spine.

"I will find you, Stormbringer."

GLOSSARY

For more information on the world of Llurien, including maps and pronunciation audio files, please visit the official site, http://www.llurien.com.

Antaria: a continent in the northern hemisphere of Llurien, usually depicted on the left/west of world maps.

Asyander: a deciduous tree growing 30-150 feet tall, used for syrup and bows.

Chaos weapons: any magical weapon left inside Everland can become corrupted so that it's powers are unpredictable.

Coiryn: the god of courage, honor, integrity, pride, dignity, protection, victory, and heroism. He's the autumn/earth god of the green sphere and one of the creators of karelia. He's the patron of warriors and rules the first month of autumn in the Court of Gods.

Coiryn Riders: named for the god of courage, these expert horsemen are a major unit of defense for almost all cities and major towns.

Daekais: one of the original seven species of Llurien but now a race of the kais species. Created by the gods of the orange sphere: deception, greed, jealousy, and fear. Their teeth and claws are poisonous. See "kais" and "Deal of the Gods" entries.

Deal of the Gods: an agreement between the gods to allow ghosts to happen, to create morkais from a male and female daekais, to give magic to the species, to grant healing powers if species create religions, and give the karelia supernatural talents to resolve matters of undead and roaming spirits.

E'Kainum: the afterlife created by the gods of the orange sphere, reserved for the evilest, whose souls are shredded into oblivion without hope of recovery.

Ever Earth: soil found in Everland and which causes anything planted in it to produce an unusual and unpredictable yield, either in volume or properties.

Ever Fiend: the Ever Fiend is rumored to rule Everland and use Ever Gates to appear on Llurien to terrorize people.

Ever Gates: portals from Llurien to Everland. They are naturally occurring but hard to detect without the Reveal Ever Gate spell. Karelia can sense them. From within Everland, they are always open, but from Llurien, a spell must be used to open one.

Everland: a supernatural land ruled by the Ever Fiend and accessed directly via Ever Gates, or indirectly via Moon Gates. Everland, and everything in it, like the Ever Fiend, is not believed to be real by most people.

Ever Pathways: another name for Everland.

Humans: the eighth species of Llurien, humans were created by all twenty-eight gods and are the most variable species in temperament and disposition. Also called Antarians after the first man and woman, Antar and Taria respectively.

Jhaikan: one of the original seven species of Llurien. Created by the gods of the blue sphere: wrath, cruelty, cunning, and domination. They stand seven to nine feet tall, have a sinuous tail and reptilian skin that can change colors at will. They are man-eaters and are synonymous with evil.

Jhaikan Staff: a quarterstaff developed and used by kryll against jhaikan, it can be disassembled into three pieces for easier transport. Blades can be made to protrude from either end like a scythe, spear, or both.

Kais: this humanoid species has two races: daekais and morkais. Aside from disposition, they are largely the same, about four feet tall with feathery wings.

Karelia: one of the original seven species of Llurien. Created by the gods of the green sphere: truth, exuberance, courage, and intuition. They need only four hours of sleep a night and have a well-developed sixth sense that varies from one to another in just what they can sense and do. Appointed by the gods to resolve supernatural disturbances.

Karelian Sword: a double-edged weapon with a sharp tip, two and a half feet long, being a half foot longer than a short sword. The hilt is long enough for the karelia to use this sword as two-handed, but larger species may use only one hand.

Kerr: an ill-manned mountain bovine with two curved horns that are used to ram anyone or anything entering its territory. Prized for milk (used for cheeses), skins, and their wool. Their waste is known to be especially smelly, resulting in the popular expression, "kerr shit."

Kona leech: a predatory vined plant in the darkshade family. It slowly feeds on the blood of creatures it captures, which it renders docile with a secretion to calm them. Victims die of starvation or dehydration, as the plant wants them to live as long as possible. The plant is mobile, moving from tree to tree and hanging over trails.

Kryll: one of the original seven species of Llurien. Created by the gods of the red sphere: curiosity, aspiration, fairness, and peace. They prefer to live in large Evenorr trees and are extremely acrobatic, athletic, and masters of weapons. Every kryll has a subject to which they devote themselves, becoming an expert.

Kryllan Hand: a magical pair of bracers over the forearms. With a word, a metal gauntlet covers the hands, allowing for hand-to-sword combat. Also a fighting style of martial arts.

Kryllan Sword: equivalent to a bastard sword.

Leisiran: the afterlife conceived by the gods of the indigo sphere, reserved for the moderately good, who enjoy a paradise for eternity.

Llorus: a large continent lying mostly on the southern hemisphere of Llurien, south of the continent Antaria.

Llurien: the planet, which has two moons.

Linganore Trees: believed to only grow in Everland in a grove surrounding the Ever Fiend's Black Tower. Black trunks and blood red leaves. The trees are sentient and can move, barring passage, trapping people, or killing them.

Lochiare: the afterlife conceived by the gods of the blue sphere, for the moderately evil, who suffer eternal torture.

Maeryndor: an afterlife conceived by the gods of the violet sphere, for the least evil, who suffer boredom everlasting.

Magician: anyone with magic talent, whether they've become a full-fledged wizard or sorcerer or not. The term can be an insult to anyone of skill and power, since they should be referred to by their proper skillset: wizard or sorcerer.

Mandeans: one of the original seven species of Llurien. Created by the gods of the indigo sphere: innocence, passion, expression, and unity. They are water dwelling and rarely seen on land except by the shore.

Moon Gates: powered by the moon, Moon Gates are portals that allow nearly instantaneous travel between two Moon Gates, which are typically controlled by Priests of Scrylyn. The gates actually use the Ever Pathways at high speeds, meaning travelers are going through Everland, but most people don't realize this.

Morkais: a race of the kais species, they resulted from the Deal of the Gods and were created by all twelve "good" gods from a male and female daekais. See "kais" entry.

Mynx: a large, maneless, carnivorous cat (some as large as a horse) that can be trained in battle tactics and bonded to its owner. Mynx can wear armor, follow commands, and communicate threats to their owner with different vocalizations.

Orb of Vessyn: a sphere located in the Vanishing Tower of Everland and which causes the tower to randomly change locations.

Poison Pond: located in Everland, the Poison Pond is believed to have killed a group of riven who entered it for unknown reasons. The waters have since turned silver and are known as the silver elixir, a potent supernatural item.

Priest: members of a religious order. Within a priesthood, clerics and healers are more specific roles than the generic term priest, which not only refers to all of them, but to those who conduct ceremonies, listen to people's problems and console them, and interpret the will of the gods for the common people, though clerics and healers can also do this. Priests are the figureheads of a religion, while clerics administrate the religion and healers heal the wounded.

Querra: one of the original seven species of Llurien. Created by the gods of the yellow sphere: inspiration, empathy, rejuvenation, and patience. Three to four feet tall, they are playful, wise, and beloved by many.

Riven: one of the original seven species of Llurien. Created by the gods of the violet sphere: haste, hate, cynicism, and sloth. Three to four feet tall and often carrying diseases.

Silver Elixir: the toxic waters of the Poison Pond in Everland. Highly prized by magicians for its supernatural properties, which augment spells. Can be used to turn ordinary weapons into Chaos Blades.

Sorcerers: the class of magician which is capable of performing magic through force of will, rather than needing a spell.

Sorelia: a corrupted race of the karelian species, they were created when the goddess of corruption, Ronkainen, read the passage about creating karelia from the Book of Creation. Sorelia look just like karelia but have more variable eye colors. They are considered malevolent.

Species: while this can refer to animals, it usually refers to the humanoid species: karelia, mandeans, querra, kryll, kais, riven, jhaikan, and humans, some of which have multiple races.

Valenders: simple spells that any magician can usually do whether they've trained to become a wizard or not (or developed their talent for sorcery).

Valendry: the art of creating magical items.

Valend wizard: magicians who failed the tests to become wizards and are not allowed to perform magic except by creating magic items, known as valendry.

Wizards: the class of magician who needs spells to work magic.

About The Author

Randy Ellefson has written fantasy fiction since his teens and is an avid world builder, having spent three decades creating Llurien, which has its own website. He has a Bachelor of Music in classical guitar but has always been more of a rocker, having released several albums and earned endorsements from music companies. He's a professional software developer and runs a consulting firm in the Washington D.C. suburbs. He loves spending time with his son and daughter when not writing, making music, or playing golf.

Connect with me online

http://www.RandyEllefson.com
http://twitter.com/RandyEllefson
http://facebook.com/RandyEllefsonAuthor

If you like this book, please help others enjoy it.

Lend it. Please share this book with others.
Recommend it. Please recommend it to friends, family, reader groups, and discussion boards
Review it. Please review the book at Goodreads and the vendor where you bought it.

JOIN THE RANDY ELLEFSON NEWSLETTER!

Subscribers receive discounts, exclusive bonus scenes, and the latest promotions and updates! A FREE digital copy of *The Ever Fiend (Talon Stormbringer)* is immediately sent to new subscribers!

www.ficiton.randyellefson.com/newsletter

Randy Ellefson Books

Talon Stormbringer

Talon is a sword-wielding adventurer who has been a thief, pirate, knight, king, and more in his far-ranging life.

The Ever Fiend
The Screaming Moragul

www.fiction.randyellefson.com/talonstormbringer

The Dragon Gate Series

Four unqualified Earth friends are magically summoned to complete quests on other worlds, unless they break the cycle – or die trying.

Volume 1: *The Dragon Gate*
Volume 2: *The Light Bringer*
Volume 3: *The Silver-Tongued Rogue*
Volume 4: *The Dragon Slayer*
Volume 5: *The Majestic Magus*

www.fiction.randyellefson.com/dragon-gate-series/

The Art of World Building

This is a multi-volume guide for authors, screenwriters, gamers, and hobbyists to build more immersive, believable worlds fans will love.

Volume 1: *Creating Life*
Volume 2: *Creating Places*
Volume 3: *Cultures and Beyond*
Volume 4: *Creating Life: The Podcast Transcripts*
Volume 5: *Creating Places: The Podcast Transcripts*
Volume 6: *Cultures and Beyond: The Podcast Transcripts*
185 Tips on World Building
The Complete Art of World Building
The Art of the World Building Workbook: Fantasy Edition
The Art of the World Building Workbook: Sci-Fi Edition

Visit www.artofworldbuilding.com for details.

Randy Ellefson Music

Instrumental Guitar

Randy has released three albums of hard rock/metal instrumentals, one classical guitar album, and an all-acoustic album. Visit http://www.music.randyellefson.com for more information, streaming media, videos, and free mp3s.

2004: *The Firebard*
2007: *Some Things Are Better Left Unsaid*
2010: *Serenade of Strings*
2010: *The Lost Art*
2013: *Now Weaponized!*
2014: *The Firebard (re-release)*